"I don't believe in your special abilities, Miss Lockhart," Santana said in that deep voice of his.

Annie shot up and crossed the short distance between her and the handsome, aggravating Santana. She reached down and placed her hand on his shoulder. There was tension in his shoulder, in his neck and the way he held his arm....

A vision immediately popped into her mind. The first thing that came to her made her twitch, and she almost drew her hand in and jumped back. She saw, with a clarity so sharp she held her breath, this gorgeous man hovering above her. Naked. The fan on her bedroom ceiling whirred slowly over his left shoulder. He had a small crescent-shaped scar on that finely sculpted shoulder. An old one. The expression on his face was... She shivered. Feral. Possessive. *Hungry.*

Dear Reader,

Writers are often told, "Write what you know." Some days that's easy. Other days…not so much. I've never been a private detective, like Lucky, and my husband has told me time and again that I can't have a gun. I don't know what he's so worried about, but it seems important to him so there's another subject on which I am not an expert. I'm certainly not psychic, like Annie, and while I have dabbled in crafty hobbies in the past, making pretty things that other people actually want is beyond me.

And still, I found myself identifying with both Lucky and Annie. Love, with all the joys and heartaches it brings, is universal. Two people who at first glance have absolutely nothing in common can, and do, discover that maybe deep down they're not so different after all.

I hope you enjoy the book!

Linda

LINDA
WINSTEAD JONES
LUCKY'S
WOMAN

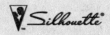

INTIMATE MOMENTS™

Published by Silhouette Books

America's Publisher of Contemporary Romance

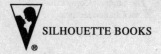 SILHOUETTE BOOKS

ISBN-13: 978-0-373-27503-8
ISBN-10:   0-373-27503-X

LUCKY'S WOMAN

Copyright © 2006 by Linda Winstead Jones

Books by Linda Winstead Jones

Silhouette Intimate Moments

Bridger's Last Stand #924
Every Little Thing #1007
*Madigan's Wife #1068
*Hot on His Trail #1097
*Capturing Cleo #1137
Secret-Agent Sheik #1142
*In Bed with Boone #1156
*Wilder Days #1203
*Clint's Wild Ride #1217
*On Dean's Watch #1234
A Touch of the Beast #1317
†Running Scared #1334
†Truly, Madly, Dangerously #1348
†One Major Distraction #1372
The Sheik and I #1420
†Lucky's Woman #1433

Silhouette Books

Love Is Murder
"Calling after Midnight"

Family Secrets
Fever

*The Sinclair Connection
†Last Chance Heroes

LINDA WINSTEAD JONES

has written more than fifty romance books in several subgenres. Historical, fairy-tale, paranormal and, of course, romantic suspense. She's won the Colorado Romance Writers Award of Excellence twice, is a three-time RITA® Award finalist and (writing as Linda Fallon) winner of the 2004 RITA® Award for paranormal romance.

Linda lives in north Alabama with her husband of thirty-four years. She can be reached via www.eHarlequin.com or her own Web site, www.lindawinsteadjones.com.

To Marge and Dave,
for all the loving support through the years.

Chapter 1

Annie came up off the bed with a gasp, one hand flying to her sweaty forehead, the other gripping the sheet beneath her. Not again. Not that same damn dream *again*. Her heart was pumping so hard and fast she could feel it, and a sheen of perspiration that wasn't normal on such a cool morning covered her face and made her lightweight pajamas stick to her skin.

She left the bed quickly—as if she could escape the dream that way—peeling off her pajamas as she walked to the master bath to turn on the shower. Standing beneath the spray with her eyes closed, she tried to imagine the dream washing away and swirling down the drain. It didn't, of course. It stayed with her much too vividly.

In the dream, a handsome man and a pretty dark-haired woman sat on a blue couch, happy for the moment. Obliviously, innocently happy and very much in love. They were bathed in a pink glow, as if their love surrounded and protected them. Their world was small, and sweet, and they saw nothing before them but years and years of love and togetherness.

All of a sudden *he* was there without warning, with a knife in his hand and an anger that colored the edges of the dream red. With that anger boiling and raging, he killed them.

Annie shampooed her short, blond hair and began to scrub as if she were washing away the blood she'd seen in her nightmare. Tears stung her eyes, but she didn't cry. She'd had the dream four nights in a row, and she didn't know what to do.

This wasn't the first time she'd had dreams that were more than dreams, but it had been a long while. She'd been so sure the aberration was over—gone—finished, once and for all. Apparently this curse or ability she'd *never* wanted had just been pushed deep. Something had caused it to rise to the surface, and she'd do whatever she had to in order to make the dreams stop.

Annie's psychic gift had been inherited from her grandmother on her mother's side. Grams had told her long ago that if she didn't exercise the ability it would eventually go away. It was no different than being naturally good at baseball but choosing not to play the game. Since being psychic hadn't done Grams any good at all, deciding not to play had been easy for Annie. For the most part, it worked. Since she didn't exercise the ability, it didn't often surface. But now and then, she had the dreams….

Last time something like this had happened, Annie had been twenty-two years old and unbelievably naive. Grams, the only person who might truly understand, had been gone three years by that time. Unable to turn to her recently divorced parents, and unsure about how her friends would react, Annie made the worst mistake of her life. She went to the police.

That wasn't a mistake she cared to repeat.

Wrapped in a towel, her short hair towel-dried and the latest dream still too closely with her, Annie went to her computer. She needed help—serious help—and she wasn't sure where to turn. She wasn't going to make the same mistake twice. It had been five years since the fiasco in Nashville, and she would not allow the heart-break and embarrassment to be repeated. She liked it here in Mercerville, Tennessee, tucked into the mountains in what had to be one of the most naturally beautiful spots in the world. She had friends here, and her business was doing well. Tourists who came here for the serenity of the mountains found her one-of-a-kind hats and handbags intriguing. They told their friends, who called and placed orders by phone. One customer at a time, the business had grown. She had two small but prosperous shops in the area—one in Mercerville and another in Wears Valley—and was thinking of opening a third in Pigeon Forge. She had a life, a *good* life, and she wasn't going to throw it away by confronting police officers who would just laugh at her.

But she had to do something. Someone had to stop this madman who'd killed two people simply because they were happy.

She keyed "private investigator" into the search engine, and scrolled down the first page, her fingers trembling. She'd be best off finding someone in the southeast, but not right in her backyard. When this was finished, she wouldn't want the person who'd helped her to be too close.

Nothing jumped out at her right away so she continued, going to the next page and scanning the names. There were so many! Who could she trust with this? Who would take care of the matter without bringing her neat little world crashing down onto her head?

On the third page it happened. A name seemed to pop off the page, brighter than the rest. It drew her eye in an unnatural way, making her heart lurch. She read the first line, which told just a little bit about the company Web site. They were based in Alabama. Close, but not too close. In an instant Annie knew without doubt she'd found someone who could help her.

The Benning Agency.

Lucky kicked his feet up on the desk in his home office, holding his ear to the phone and listening to it ring on the other end. One, two, three rings. He was wondering where Sadie could be so early on a Monday morning, and trying to decide if he wanted to leave a message on the machine or not, when someone answered.

"Helloooo."

Great. Just what he needed. "Hi. Is your mommy—"

"My name's Grant," the overly enthusiastic young voice proclaimed.

"Yes, I know. I—"

"I have a baby sister," Grant said enthusiastically. "She's new. Her name is Reagan."

"Yes, I—"

"I like her, but sometimes she stinks."

There should be a law against three-year-olds answering the telephone. "This is Uncle Lucky," he said quickly and precisely.

"Hey! You gave me a toy gun for my birthday!"

"Yes, I did. Can I—"

"Daddy only lets me play with my toy gun sometimes, not always. When I'm the Incredible Spiderman I don't need a gun because I have my spidey powers."

Lucky sighed, and gave up on his hopes of talking to Sadie anytime soon. "No, Spiderman doesn't—"

"The *Incredible* Spiderman!" the kid corrected with enthusiasm. And then he started making what were probably supposed to be spidey sounds.

"Can I speak to your mother?" Lucky spoke loudly to be heard above the din.

"You didn't say *please*."

"Please."

"She's changing a diaper right now. I have a baby sister! Her name is Reagan. Sometimes she stinks."

Grant could be amusing, but he was getting repetitive and that was never a good thing. "If you'll take the phone to your mother, I'll bring you some candy next time I visit."

Grant paused for a split second. "M&M's?"

"Whatever you want."

Suddenly Grant's voice was distant, as the kid held

the portable phone away from his mouth and called, "Mommy! It's Unca Lucky!"

A few moments later, Sadie uttered a breathless "Hello?"

Without responding to the greeting, Lucky said, "You let a kid who's barely three years old answer the phone?"

His old partner laughed. Man, there were days when he missed that laugh more than he dared to admit. "He taught himself. What can I say?"

"You can start by telling him not to give his name over the phone until he knows who he's talking to."

Sadie sighed. "Thanks for letting me know. I'll take care of it. Nobody told me two kids would be ten times as much work as one. Twice as much I expected, that makes sense, but…I swear, Lucky, I have completely lost control."

Sadie had lost control the minute she'd hooked up with Truman McCain, but that was an argument she didn't want to hear. "I know the feeling. Heather left a couple of days ago." Saturday afternoon, to be exact.

"Why?" Sadie managed to sound outraged, even though she had never liked Heather and hadn't been shy about saying so.

"She said I'm commitment phobic."

"Well," Sadie said, less outrage in her voice, "you are. I mean, you and Heather were together for what, five months? That's the longest I've ever known you to stay with one woman."

"Siding with the enemy?"

"You didn't love her, and I can tell you're not all that

upset that she's gone. You're just peeved because she left first. She wasn't right for you, anyway. She was like all your other women—drop-dead gorgeous and shallow and temporary and not too smart. Maybe you should let me pick the next one." There was more than a touch of humor in her voice as she made that ridiculous suggestion.

Lucky heard Grant's insistent voice in the background.

"You will not bring this child candy next time you visit," Sadie declared, the tone of her voice changing dramatically. "Do you have any idea what Grant's like when he ingests too much sugar?"

"Oh, yeah. I was at the birthday party, remember?" Lucky hadn't missed any of Grant's birthday parties. Sadie's husband, Truman, who was now sheriff of the small county where they lived their chaotic and ideal life, had once been suspicious of Lucky's motives where Sadie was concerned. In nearly four years Truman had come to accept that his wife and the man who had once been her partner were just friends. The best of friends, but still…just friends.

It was only on the bad days that Lucky acknowledged that he had once been a little bit in love with Sadie. On the worst of days, he wondered if he still was.

"When are you going to come see the baby?" Sadie asked. "She's beautiful."

"I hear she stinks." In spite of the bad mood he'd been in when he'd made this call, Lucky smiled widely.

"I have air freshener. Just don't wear your best suit."

"Warning noted."

"So," she continued, "when?"

"I don't know." He wasn't very good company for anyone these days. "I've been spending a few days at home, and Cal has me training a handful of new guys this week. After that, who knows?"

The Benning Agency had grown since Sadie's departure. Flynn Benning still owned the agency, but he was rarely around anymore. He had his hands full with a new family and a new career. Teaching, of all things. Cal ran the show, and there were now more than twenty agents—men and women—employed by the once small agency. They were thinking of branching out and opening an office in Nashville, or maybe Atlanta. It had even been mentioned that Lucky might head up a Nashville office, since he kept a house less than an hour away. Most of the others lived near the main office in rural Alabama, but Lucky liked to get away from it all when he wasn't working a case.

He'd been asking himself lately—did he want to head up the Nashville office, if it came to that? It sounded an awful lot like a real job.

"You have to be here for Thanksgiving," Sadie said. "The new house will be finished by then, and I have great holiday plans."

"Like you don't have your hands full enough as it is. What happened to ten times the work with two kids?"

"It'll be a lot of work, it'll be a huge hassle. I know that. But I want a big, traditional Thanksgiving in my new house," Sadie insisted. "And you have to be here. It just wouldn't be the same without you."

Lucky hated to admit that he needed anything, but he needed Sadie in his life. He even needed Grant and

Truman and the new baby. The situation was almost ideal. He could visit whenever he wanted, share their perfect little family life for a while and then leave the chaos and go back to his well-ordered life, where nothing ever stunk and he never had to say please to get what he wanted.

Crap. Maybe Heather was right.

"I gotta go," Sadie said too quickly. "Spiderman is climbing on the kitchen table."

In the background, Grant protested, "The *Incredible* Spiderman!"

"Thanksgiving!" Sadie ordered, and then she severed the connection.

Thanksgiving was less than two months away. He really should visit before then to see the new baby and take a present for smelly little Reagan, and maybe he would. But he suddenly hated the idea of showing up alone again, to be a fifth wheel in Sadie's family life. Or worse, showing up with a woman who was exactly as Sadie had described. Gorgeous, shallow…and temporary.

When the phone rang he automatically checked the caller ID to see if Sadie—or maybe even Grant—had decided to call him back. But the number on the display was another familiar one.

Lucky answered with a crisp "Santana."

Cal didn't bother with niceties. "I've got a job for you."

"I thought I was going to be training all week." His suitcase was already in the trunk of his car, and he'd been planning to head south within the hour.

"You hate training," Cal said, and it was a true enough statement. "Besides, this won't even take a full day, I promise. You can be here torturing the new guys by tomorrow afternoon, no problem. Meet with the woman this afternoon or tomorrow morning, listen to what she has to say, tell her we'll do what we can but it's really not our specialty and get out. Easy, right?"

The jobs they thought would be *easy* always seemed to be the most difficult. "Why don't you just tell her over the phone that we can't help her?"

"I tried that. She's very persistent."

"What kind of case is this, exactly?"

Cal hesitated.

"Dammit, Calhoun…"

"Okay, she's a kook. She had some sort of vision or something, and she claims she knows details about a murder but she doesn't want to go to the police."

Of course she didn't. The police had probably had their fill of the local *psychic*. "You've got to be kidding me."

"She's a paying kook. She won't rest easy until someone listens to her, and I figure she lives a couple of hours, maybe a little more, from your house. Call her, set up a meeting, get a statement and—hell—pacify her and get out as quick as you can."

Maybe taking a statement from a kook would be more fun than sitting here staring out the window and fuming. Not because Heather was gone. Sadie had been too right when she'd said that he was pissed not because she'd left, but because he hadn't been the one to do the leaving.

Everyone always disappointed him in the end. Family, friends, partners…lovers.

He grabbed a pad of paper and a silver pen. "Give me the kook's address and phone number."

* * *

Annie put the finishing touches on a special-order hat, placed it on her head and viewed the results in the mirror. She couldn't help but smile. There was no accounting for tastes, but Teri Boyd was a good customer, and she was paying well for this hat and the matching bag. It wasn't as if they'd actually be displayed in either of her shops. Annie's Closet was trendy and her customers had fun browsing among the unexpected and unique. But this hat, feathers and all, was perhaps *too* unique. Looking at her reflection, Annie rearranged the silk sash. Maybe the hat was for a costume party, and Teri had neglected to tell her so.

The doorbell rang, and she jumped. Thanks to the dream, she'd been jumpy all day. Thank goodness she could work at home, when she wanted to. Each of her shops was capably run by a manager and a handful of part-timers, most of whom worked at Annie's Closet simply so they could claim an employee discount.

Her hand was on the doorknob when she remembered to ask, "Who is it?" The door was solid wood. She really should have a peephole, but she'd never gotten around to having one put in.

For a moment no one answered, and then a deep male voice grumbled, "I thought you were psychic. Why do you have to ask who's at the door?"

Had to be someone from the Benning Agency. No one else—and she did mean *no one*—knew about her too-real dreams. Annie opened the door slowly and looked up at what had to be the most gorgeous man she'd ever seen up close and personal. The man on her doorstep had dark hair—almost black but not quite—which had recently been neatly trimmed. Extremely prominent on his handsome face were amber eyes which were striking and powerful. He had a sharp jawline that looked as if it wouldn't dare to sprout stubble, humorless, perfectly shaped lips and wide shoulders.

He wore an expensive black suit that looked as if it had been made for that fine body. Even the white dress shirt seemed perfectly fitted. If the tie wasn't slightly loose and crooked, she'd think him too perfect to be real. She detected a hint of Hispanic heritage in his features, which was at odds with his honeyed Southern accent.

As he stared down at her, a smile tugged at his lips. "Nice hat," he said.

Annie yanked the wide-brimmed and much-festooned hat from her head. "I thought you would call first."

"Sorry. I figured you'd know I was coming."

He didn't believe her. Well, what had she expected?

"Come in." She took a step back and invited him into her home, a very nice cabin with a fantastic view of the mountains from the back deck. The cabin was small, but just right for one person. The great room doubled as a work area, on most days. The kitchen was small, but functional. Her bedroom was on the main floor, as was a smaller spare bedroom, and there was an open loft for extra guests, if she ever had them. It was used for storing supplies, most of the time.

When her visitor was inside and she'd closed the

door behind him, she offered her hand. "Annie Lockhart. Thank you for coming."

He looked at her hand for a moment before taking it and shaking briefly and professionally. "Lucky Santana. Benning Agency. I dearly hate it when someone wastes my time."

He obviously thought this trip was a waste of time. "Well, then, I'll be as brief as possible," she told him.

Santana's eyes raked over the cabin quickly, taking in everything with an emotionless and seemingly bored precision. In the great room many of her supplies were scattered here and there—feathers and netting and sequins, felt and silk flowers—but there were two empty chairs sitting just a few feet apart, and they claimed them. Santana then turned his inquisitive amber eyes to her.

While he watched her with calculating eyes, Annie wished she'd chosen a different outfit this morning. The worn hip-hugger jeans were comfortable, and the beaded T-shirt was one of her favorites, but at the moment she'd give almost anything if her belly button was fully covered and her shirt didn't cling to her breasts. Shoes would be better than the toe ring—which was all she wore on her feet. This man just studied her too damn *hard*.

"A man and woman from just south of Mercerville were murdered a couple of months ago," she began. "Well, on the news the sheriff said it was a murder-suicide, but he's wrong. There was no suicide. A man broke into their house and…" She shook her head as an image from the dream assaulted her. "He murdered them both."

"Who is *he*?" Santana asked, still openly suspicious.

"I don't know. In my dream it was like I was in his head. I couldn't see what he looked like."

"In your dream," he repeated without emotion.

"Surely Mr. Calhoun explained to you why—"

"Yes," Santana interrupted. "He explained that you're a psychic of some sort, but he didn't tell me what you expect us to do for you. What did the sheriff say when you told him about your dream?"

She tried not to look guilty. "I didn't tell the sheriff, and I won't. Surely Mr. Calhoun told you that I don't want to go to the authorities. That's the reason I called your company."

"Yeah, he told me. I just wanted to hear the 'why' from you."

"The 'why' is very simple. They won't believe me."

"Miss Lockhart," Santana said in that deep and emotionless voice of his, "*I* don't believe you."

"I'm paying you to believe," she snapped, and then she reined her temper in. "Look, I can tell you what I know about the killer and how he killed those poor people. Then you can look for concrete evidence, find the killer and turn him in. You can be the hero, he'll be off the streets as he should be and no one needs to know that I had anything to do with it."

"Miss Lockhart…"

"Annie, please."

He lifted one eyebrow, just slightly. "I don't want to waste your money or my time chasing after a dream. Maybe you should, uh, see a doctor about your nightmares. Medication is a good thing."

For a long moment, Annie didn't move. She'd been so certain the Benning Agency was the one. The name had popped off the page, hadn't it? She'd felt such a great relief after she'd talked to Mr. Calhoun on the phone early this morning. And now this man was all but calling her crazy. How could she convince him that she needed his help?

Annie could keep her psychic gift dormant most of the time, but just like the time in Nashville, the dreams didn't seem to care if she practiced or not. The vivid nightmares were bad enough, but when they came—as they had done this past week and as they had five years ago—they didn't come alone. Waking and sleeping, she knew things she shouldn't. If she kept herself busy, she could push the clairvoyance to the back of her mind. But when she concentrated, when she cleared her mind and reached for that which she shouldn't know, her mind didn't stay clear for long. Sometimes she didn't have to reach; the knowledge was just *there*. She saw images…she heard voices. Until the man who'd killed the couple was caught, the problem wouldn't go away.

She cleared her mind now, pushing away the everyday thoughts that had kept her sane in the days past so she could convince this man to help her. "He killed this couple because they were happy," she said, gathering as much calm as she could. "He stalked them, he watched their every move for…months." She whispered the last word, as it came to her. "He loved and hated and envied them, and then when he got tired of watching, he murdered them."

"Miss Lockhart…"

"Even if I dared to go to the authorities, the sheriff won't listen to me," Annie said frantically. "He and anyone else I go to will write me off as a nutcase, and word will get around, and pretty soon everyone in town will be whispering behind my back. Some of them will wonder if maybe it's true that I have unnatural abilities, but more of them will laugh. Worse, some of them will think that if I know anything I shouldn't, then I had something to do with the murders. I like my life as it is, Mr. Santana, but I can't just ignore what I saw and let it go. I had the dreams for a *reason*. I picked your agency for a reason." She didn't realize that her voice had been rising with each word until she almost shouted the last one.

"This isn't the sort of case my agency normally takes. Perhaps you should call someone—"

Annie shot up and crossed the short distance between her and the handsome and aggravating Lucky Santana. She reached down and placed her hand on his shoulder. There was immediate tension in his shoulder, in his neck and the way he held his arm.

She didn't really know how to call upon her gift when she needed it. During the few times in her life when this had happened she'd done her best to cut herself off from the unnatural ability, not call it up. Annie's mother had been so embarrassed by her own mother's abilities. She'd hated the fact that she was the daughter of a freak. The very idea that her daughter might be afflicted as well had been difficult for her. She'd insisted that Annie not pursue the life of a psychic, and her argument was a good one. Grams had practiced; she'd practiced a lot. And it hadn't done her a damn bit of good.

From her limited past experience she understood that contact would be a good thing. She already knew Lucky Santana didn't believe her.

A vision immediately popped into her mind. The first thing that came to her made her twitch, and she almost drew her hand in and jumped back. She saw, with a clarity so sharp she held her breath, this gorgeous man hovering above her. Naked. The fan on her bedroom ceiling whirred slowly over his left shoulder. He had a small crescent-shaped scar on that finely sculpted shoulder. An old one. The expression on his face was—she shivered—feral. Possessive. *Hungry.* Was she seeing what some hidden part of her wanted to see, or was this what was meant to be? What *might* be?

She forced herself to reach beyond the vision for something else. Something she could actually use. "I'm sorry," she said softly. "I usually try to stop these visions, not bring them on. I don't have any control over what comes to me."

"I see," Santana said, his voice dripping with sarcasm and disbelief.

Annie forced herself to relax. Given what she'd just seen, she should send this man away as quickly as possible. Maybe the Benning Agency wasn't the one after all. Maybe she needed to start all over. Lucky Santana was a heartbreaker, and the last thing she needed was to get involved with a man who wouldn't stay. "The redhead is right, you are commitment phobic," she said.

Santana flinched slightly beneath her hand, but didn't shove her away. He still wasn't convinced.

"A new office?" The longer she worked at seeing inside this man, the easier it became. She relaxed, a little. What she needed to convince him that she wasn't a nut would come—or it wouldn't. She had to trust herself, just this once. "You don't think you'll like that sort of work, spending all that time in what's basically an administrative role, but once you get settled you'll find you like it more than you'd imagined you could." She cocked her head to one side and looked into his amazing amber eyes.

He was dressed conservatively, and his haircut was traditional. But there was nothing conservative about those eyes. They were fire and ice. Passion and indifference.

Everything about him was cool, even his voice as he said, "If you're trying to convince me you can read minds, you're doing a poor job. You haven't told me anything Cal couldn't have mentioned over the phone."

"The man you work for would share such personal information with a potential client?"

"If it means yanking my chain, yeah." He stood, and her hand dropped away. "I enjoyed the drive over, so I'm going to tell Cal not to bill you for this call. Miss Lockhart, I do advise you to speak with a doctor or a therapist as soon as possible."

Lucky Santana was almost to the door. He was, in fact, reaching for the doorknob. If he walked out, what would she do? Maybe the Benning Agency would send someone else, but Santana was the one to help her—she knew it. She felt it. What could she say to make him understand?

"You don't really love her," she called as Santana

opened the door. He stopped, turned to look at her with blazing eyes and slammed the door shut.

"You don't really love her," Annie said again, more softly this time. And then she began to hum the tune that popped into her head.

Chapter 2

It wasn't an easy song to hum, and Annie Lockhart couldn't carry a tune. And still, Lucky immediately recognized the song. "Sexy Sadie."

He'd been very careful to keep his occasional romantic musings about Sadie to himself. No one knew how he felt—how he sometimes thought he might feel. Not even Sadie. For a moment Lucky was blindingly angry. Somehow the men he worked with did know, and this was an elaborate setup intended to embarrass him. A practical joke. And then he looked into Annie Lockhart's eyes and saw the unshed tears.

If this was a joke, she wasn't in on it.

Annie Lockhart was blond, blue-eyed and average height. Maybe a bit taller than average, thanks to those long legs encased in faded denim. The couple of inches of skin he could see between the waistband and the hem of her shirt, which was adorned with a little sparkly stuff, was shapely enough to draw any man's eye. She was slender—but not thin. Nice build, but nothing eye-popping. Quirky, even without the hat. Her blond hair was soft and straight, but the cut was uneven and purposely ragged, giving her a tousled look. And she hadn't looked squarely at him since she'd told him he "didn't love her."

"It's…it's trust," Lockhart said in a lowered voice, when she finished humming. "You've confused trust and love, which is easy enough to do, I suppose."

Lucky took a few steps into the room, moving closer so he could see her face. He didn't believe in psychic abilities, but he did believe in instincts. He had pretty damn good instincts himself, honed over the years to a fine edge. Maybe in some part of her brain that she didn't understand, Annie Lockhart had put the pieces of this murder puzzle together and come up with answers she couldn't explain. Images from television, details from the newspaper, gossip…all pieces of a puzzle that had led her to believe she knew something she didn't. A couple days of investigation, if that, should prove that all her suppositions were wrong.

And the bit about Sadie? He wasn't ready to go there just yet.

"I'll give you two days, Miss Lockhart."

She closed her eyes and took a deep breath, in obvious relief. "Thank you," she whispered.

"Don't thank me yet," Lucky said sharply. "I think you're full of crap, and I'll be more than happy to prove it and then send you the bill." The Benning Agency didn't come cheap, but handling financial concerns was Cal's job—not Lucky's. "I'll need to find a hotel room...."

"Oh, I've taken care of that," the blonde said lightly. "It's a bed-and-breakfast, actually. You'll be much more comfortable there than you would be in a hotel, and it's just down the road."

Lucky thrust his hands in his pants pockets—so he wouldn't strangle the client. "You made a reservation for me? Before I got here and agreed to take the job?"

"Instead of being irritable, you should thank me. This is a very busy time of year in the area, with the leaves changing colors and the weather turning cool. I didn't know who Mr. Calhoun would send, of course, so just give Kristie my name when you check in."

Since he had agreed to take her case, Annie Lockhart had relaxed considerably. She smiled a little, and the tears in her pretty blue eyes had dried, he noticed, as she gave him directions to the bed-and-breakfast down the hill. She was cute, but not his type. The women he dated were always beautiful. Not just cute, not merely pretty. He was drawn to women who turned heads in a major way. This woman was pretty enough, but she probably had never entered a room and immediately garnered every man's attention—unless she sauntered in wearing a ridiculous hat like the one she'd been wearing when she'd opened the door.

His gaze skimmed her from head to toe—not for the first time—and lingered on the toes. The toenails were painted pink, and she wore one toe ring. A yellow flower. He'd bet his last dollar she had a tattoo. Some-where. No, she was definitely not his type.

Annie Lockhart gave a brief and accurate description of the bed-and-breakfast where he'd apparently be staying. He remembered passing the large, old house on the way in. It was less than five minutes away.

Suddenly he couldn't wait to get out of this cabin. "I'll check into my room and call the office. In the morning we'll get—"

"Tonight," she interrupted. "We need to get started tonight."

"Why?"

Suddenly she looked vulnerable again, too young and too naive to be involved in discussions of murder. "The dreams won't stop unless I'm doing all I can to stop this killer. I can't have those dreams again tonight. I just can't. Come back after you check into your room and make your phone calls. I'll cook supper for us, and we can get started." She took a deep breath. "Please."

"All right, Ms. Lockhart."

"Call me Annie," she said, not for the first time. "If we're going to be working together…" She shrugged her shoulders, and for some reason she shifted her glance so that she was looking away from him and out a small window, even though there wasn't much to see beyond those particular panes of glass. After a moment, she forced her gaze back in his direction.

He should invite her to call him Lucky, but he hesi-tated. He was already too close to liking Annie Lockhart for some reason, and the last thing he needed was to get involved with a kooky chick who wore extravagant hats and thought she was psychic. "I'll check back with you in a couple of hours," he said, turning away and heading—again—for the door. He really should get in his car, head for home and call Cal from there.

"Thank you, Lucky," Annie called as he opened the door on a wonderfully cool afternoon. "I really don't know what I'd do if you refused to help."

And just like that, he was trapped. He'd never been able to turn his back on a woman in trouble. Maybe he had some sort of sick hero complex. Maybe he needed a doctor and some serious medication just as much as *psychic* Annie did. He could only hope that this time being a hero didn't lead to complete, utter disaster.

Annie felt the urge to make fried chicken and mashed potatoes for supper, along with green peas and apple crisp. She didn't cook often but she *could* cook, and having company—even if that company was a reluctant P.I. who thought she was crazy—brought out the homebody in her. Her mother had taught her the ways of the kitchen, hoping such skills would lead to a happy domestic life for her only child. That had been before divorce had soured Penny Lockhart's views on love and marriage. The lessons had ended long ago, but Annie still remembered how to cook.

Divorce, after nearly twenty-five years of marriage, had definitely soured Penny Lockhart's opinions on love, and it hadn't done much for Annie's perceptions, either. She'd always known all was not perfect with her parents, but she hadn't expected they'd call it quits after such a long time. Her father had remarried quickly, and had more children. Two boys, to be precise. It was odd, having half brothers so much younger. Since she didn't see her father and his new family often, it wasn't exactly a problem. It was simply odd.

Her mother, on the other hand, visited often. Too often, to be honest. She had no qualms about jumping in her new electric-blue sports car and driving from Florida to Tennessee, almost always arriving unannounced.

These days Annie barely recognized the woman who had taught her to cook and clean and become a good wife. There would be no more marriage for Penny. She had completely embraced the life of a middle-aged single woman. She took dance lessons and was learning to play the guitar. She dated. She flirted with men half her age, and with men old enough to be her father. She dyed her hair. Red one day, blond the next. She'd lost thirty pounds, and often wore clothing intended for women thirty years younger.

Mid-fifties did not mean matronly for Penny Lockhart.

Annie could only hope that her mother didn't make an appearance while Lucky Santana was here. How on earth would she explain him away? She certainly couldn't tell her mother the truth. Heaven forbid.

She didn't want her mother to know the psychic gift had reappeared. She'd freak, just as she had when as a child Annie had had nightmares about illness and accidents that too often came to pass within days. Why couldn't she dream of winning the lottery?

By the time Lucky returned to the cabin, supper was ready. Annie had cleared a long worktable in the great room and set out notebooks and an assortment of pens.

She was partial to the purple one, but she'd bet Lucky Santana wouldn't dare take notes in anything other than blue or black.

He remained skeptical, suspicious of her every word. It didn't matter. Eventually he would believe her. She was pretty sure he wouldn't be happy about discovering that psychic ability was real. He liked his world neat and tidy, and to have his beliefs turned upside down would not be pleasant.

With any luck, his work would chase this unwanted return of her ability away, and she could return to her simple, uncomplicated, ordinary life, in which she didn't dream of murderers or have very crisp visions of naked men in her bed.

Lucky ate as if he enjoyed the meal she'd prepared. The apple crisp went over especially well. He continued to hold much of himself back, but Annie didn't take it personally. That was his nature. He wasn't one to give his trust easily—or often. Something in his past had made him leery of getting too close to anyone—and to be honest, she needed no special gifts in order to be certain of that. She didn't know what might've happened to make him so wary, and she didn't try to see. That would be an invasion of privacy, and he was a very private person.

Besides, trying to tap deeply into her abnormal ability really wore her out. Sometimes she ended up with a headache, or double vision. Seeing what she shouldn't sapped her energy. Another reason to be rid of the nuisance.

Her newly hired P.I. relaxed a little when they moved

to the great room and the work area she'd set up. They pulled chairs to the worktable and Lucky grabbed a notebook. He reached past her purple pen to a black one—naturally.

"I'll tell you about the dreams, and you write it all down." She gestured with waving fingers.

"I'd prefer to start with the facts of the case," he responded sharply. "You do have the facts, don't you?"

"We're starting with the dreams," she insisted. The best way to rid herself of the memory of those dreams was to get them out, right? By telling him all about the nightmares, she'd be handing them over to someone else. Facts could come later.

His response was a very subtle lifting of his dark eyebrows. Would he walk out now? He wanted to. Well, he obviously didn't want to be here, and that was basically the same thing.

She'd never met anyone quite like him, and she'd known it the moment he walked into her house. There was a toughness to him, a distance, an edge she could not entirely explain. He was very big on enforcing the rules, unless, of course, he was the one breaking them. No one told him what to do, least of all a small, frightened woman.

But in the end he put pen to paper and said, "Fine. We'll do this your way. Tell me about your dreams."

Annie's thoughts were jumbled, so disconnected that for a while the notes Lucky took didn't mean much of anything. As he had imagined earlier, they looked like pieces to a large, complicated puzzle, and from what he could tell, none of the pieces fit together.

After more than half an hour, though, he began to get a clearer picture.

According to Annie's dreams, the killer had spied on his chosen couple for a long time, moving closer and closer each time. He'd stalked them; he'd taken pictures and broken into their home in order to steal a few personal items they'd never missed. Near the end he'd introduced himself to them, and they hadn't seen the threat in him—not until he'd pulled a knife and stabbed his female victim. The male—the husband—had been shot, and his wound had been made to look self-inflicted. A first-rate investigative team probably would've found holes in the carefully staged scene, but in a rural area where there hadn't been a murder in many years, it was easy for the investigators to simply accept what they saw.

Of course, this was assuming that what Annie was telling him was true, and not the product of an overactive imagination. It wouldn't be tough to confirm or disprove what she was telling him.

As Lucky took notes, he wondered: If this scenario Annie presented was correct, how had the killer overpowered two people and still managed to stage the scene as he wanted without signs of a struggle? Drugs were the most likely answer, and he wondered if anyone had run a tox screen on the victims. Depending on the circumstances and the availability of state resources, maybe. Maybe not.

After almost an hour, Annie sighed with a deep, complete tiredness. Lucky had been so intent on taking his own notes he hadn't noticed that his client had gone very pale, and her hands shook slightly. Closer examination revealed that her eyes were unfocused and tired. No, beyond tired.

"Are you all right?" Lucky set his pen aside and closed his notebook.

"Not really," Annie said, and then she attempted a laugh that was weak and tremulous. "The dreams haven't been pleasant, as you can imagine, and telling them in all detail just makes them seem real again. It's almost as if I'm living it again, as I relate what I remember." She swayed in her chair and then gripped the edge of the table to steady herself. After a moment, she placed her forehead on the table and took a long, deep breath. "Maybe this wasn't such a good idea," she said weakly.

Lucky muttered a curse and rounded the table. Annie looked as if she might fall out of her chair at any moment, and that wouldn't do. If she was putting on an act, it was a damn good one. If she wasn't...

He preferred not to think about that possibility too intently. "Come on." He helped Annie to her feet, steadying her. She felt fragile beneath his hands, soft and tiny and breakable. He liked his women the way he liked his guns—solid and dependable. Annie Lockhart was neither.

But she was a client, and she looked as if she was on the verge of falling apart.

"Enough for tonight," he said. "Get a good night's sleep, and we'll go over the notes tomorrow afternoon." After he'd had a chance to check the facts of her so-called visions and see if she'd told him anything that wasn't common knowledge. He didn't think she was lying to him. Not exactly. Maybe she'd read about these unfortunate deaths, and her overactive imagination had supplied the rest. That didn't explain the bit about Sadie, but there had to be a logical explanation for that, too.

He'd find that explanation, sooner or later. Cal wouldn't stoop so low even if he did know something he shouldn't, but Sean Murphy… This sort of prank was right up Murphy's alley. Lucky tried to recall if he'd ever said too much, after one too many drinks at the end of a tough job. Nothing came to him, but maybe later.

Dante? No, even if Dante knew he wouldn't tell. Had to be Murphy. Nerds were not to be trusted.

Lucky led Annie into the bathroom off the hallway. She sat on the lid of the commode, while he grabbed a handy washcloth and ran some cool water. With the damp washcloth in hand, he knelt before her and gently wiped her face. No makeup, he noted as he ran the washcloth over her cheek. The flawless complexion was real.

She closed her eyes and allowed him to tend to her, for a moment. He saw and felt her breathing change, as she began to regain her energy. He lowered the washcloth to her neck, and she tilted her head back while he wiped the length of her throat. Maybe Annie wasn't gorgeous, but she had a fine, slender throat. Everything about her was feminine, in a very different way from the women he was usually attracted to.

As he cooled her throat with the washcloth, she smiled. "It's good that you're here," she said softly.

"I'm not so sure about that," he responded honestly.

Annie's smile widened. "You'll see."

He didn't like the way she said that, as if she knew something he didn't.

Since she no longer looked as if she might fall apart, he dropped the washcloth into the sink and stood, then moved away from her. Fortunately, this was a good-sized bathroom, and he wasn't forced to remain too close to her.

Her eyes—bluer than ever, it seemed—looked at him with an odd mix of fearlessness and innocence. "I'm not lying."

Lucky sighed. "I know."

"I'm not crazy, either," she added crisply.

As far as Lucky was concerned, the jury on that one was still out. "I'll come by tomorrow after lunch."

Annie stood, steady and much stronger than she'd been just a few minutes ago, and passed by too closely as she made her way to the door. Lucky found himself holding his breath as she walked past him and her arm brushed against his.

"Maybe you'll believe me tomorrow," she said with confidence. "I'm sorry to be the one to shake your reality, but…well, maybe you'll believe me tomorrow. I think it's up to us to find him, and we can. I know we can." She sounded less than confident as she made this statement.

In the hallway, she turned away from the den and the front door and headed for what he assumed was her bedroom. A few minutes ago she'd looked to be on the verge of breakdown, but now her stride was steady and even. There was a hint of a womanly sway in her walk. Just enough to make everything in him tighten.

"Let yourself out," she called lightly. "I'll see you tomorrow."

Lucky was immediately incensed. "You hardly know me. We met a few hours ago, and now you're instructing me to let myself out? Have you lost your mind? Sorry, wrong question to ask."

She turned, and even in the dimly lit hallway he could see her smile. "You're gruff, and skeptical, and occasionally rude. You have little respect for women, even though you claim to like them well enough. I don't think you like me very much. At the very least, I confuse you. You're slow to give your friendship or your trust, and...with good reason, I suppose." She sighed deeply.

"But you don't have a dishonest bone in your body. I have nothing to fear by asking you to let yourself out. I don't even have to remind you to lock the front door, because I know you will."

"You don't know me," Lucky insisted.

Annie turned away and continued her slow, tired, annoyingly sexy walk to her bedroom. "Lucky Santana, I know you better than you know you."

Annie stripped off her clothes, pulled on an oversize T-shirt that had Drama Queen emblazoned across the front and fell into bed, exhausted. A moment later she heard the front door open and close, and she knew Lucky was gone for the night.

Calling up all those memories of two violent deaths had drained her. She had known the task would be unpleasant and difficult, but until her head had begun to swim and she'd looked across the table to see two Luckys as her vision doubled, she hadn't known *how* difficult.

Twice in her adult life, this inherited ability had surfaced in spite of her refusal to accept and hone it. In Nashville, as now, a murder that might've gone unsolved had been the crux of the problem. The dreams were bad enough, but they didn't come alone. They came with draining, uncontrollable, unwanted glimpses into the minds and hearts of others. It was as if the dreams unlocked a gate bursting through the defenses she'd so carefully constructed.

Maybe once she completed this mission—if that's what it was—the visions would cease again, for a while. Being tortured with vivid and all-too-true nightmares, and suffering from unwanted flashes of precognition once every four or five years, was doable, she supposed.

Annie sank into her soft mattress, relaxing completely. She'd done all she could to find the truth, so maybe tonight she wouldn't dream about the murdered couple. That would be nice. Maybe instead of death she'd dream about life. Maybe she'd dream about Lucky.

It had been a long time since she'd found herself face-to-face with a man she was attracted to. True, she wasn't his type—and he wasn't hers. Gorgeous or not, he was stodgy and conservative, and he liked his life neat and orderly and without surprise. She was too peculiar for him, even without the psychic ability. She was creative; he was logical—and she suspected he was quite the control freak. They probably didn't like any of the same movies or books.

But there was *something* between them—something besides a creepy killer. Chemistry. Hormones. One lonely person sensing another and reaching out in a primal, unmistakable way.

Lucky would never think of himself as lonely, but in his own way he was every bit as lonely as she was.

Too tired to think clearly any longer, Annie drifted toward sleep. As she fell into a slumber she remembered what it had felt like when Lucky had taken her arm, when he'd gently wiped her face and neck. And she recalled the vision of him hovering above her, naked and possessive. Her fingers moved along the sheet, tracing the scar she had not yet touched.

And when she dreamed, the images were not of death, but of life at its finest.

Lucky dialed Murphy's cell number as he stepped out of his car. The bed-and-breakfast that would be home for the next day or two was well-lit and eerily old-fashioned. He half expected a Southern belle in a hoop skirt to saunter onto the porch to greet him, maybe with a mint julep in hand.

Murphy answered on the second ring. "What's up?" he asked.

"Nothing much." Lucky sat in a rocking chair on the porch, since the cell signal here was clear and strong. "Did Cal tell you much about this case?"

Murphy laughed lightly. "The kook? Apparently she was very persistent on the telephone. Cal said you could handle her, though. Will you be here tomorrow? The new guys are even greener than the last batch, though there are one or two who have promise."

"No, I won't be there tomorrow. I'm sticking around here for a couple of days, with the kook."

There was a long moment of silence, followed by a disbelieving "You are?" And then a moment later, "Why?"

Lucky was glad Murphy couldn't see his smile. "I think maybe she's for real."

Again, there was that small, meaningful pause. Murphy probably wore his own huge grin, thinking he'd pulled one over on Lucky. But instead of egging Lucky on in his newfound belief, he exploded with a crisp "You're kidding me, right? No, this is all wrong. You're a rock, man. You can't go flaky on me. I'm going to tell Cal to order you home ASAP, you hear me? If you start seeing auras and…and *meditating*…"

"Hold on," Lucky ordered. "I'm just pulling your leg."

"Oh." There was a lot of relief in that one syllable. "So why are you staying? I get it," Murphy continued before Lucky had a chance to respond. "She's, like, gorgeous, right?"

"Pretty enough," Lucky conceded.

"Oh." Again there was a world of meaning in that one word. Lucky Santana didn't go for women who were simply *pretty enough*. "Don't stay there too long," Murphy continued. "I have some new, kickin' toys."

Murphy was Benning's computer and gadget expert. His toys were always interesting. "A couple of days, maybe."

"Cool. Be careful."

Lucky flipped his phone closed and headed for the door. Not Murphy, then. So who had told pretty enough Annie Lockhart that he'd once had the major hots for Sadie?

That was the true mystery, one he was determined to solve before he headed south to kick someone's sorry ass for playing this practical joke on him.

Chapter 3

After a restless night filled with disjointed dreams that made no sense, Lucky was awakened by a knock on his door and a cheerful "Good morning! Breakfast is ready!" He glanced at the bedside clock and growled low in his throat.

He recognized the overly bright voice as belonging to the woman who owned and operated this bed-and-breakfast. Somehow he always associated elderly women with the job of landlady, especially in an older home like this one, but Kristie Bentley and her husband, Stu, were a young couple—probably not even thirty years old. They were newlyweds, married less than a year, and they were both attractive and friendly. And much too freakin' cheerful.

Lucky crawled out of bed, quickly pulled on a pair

of pants and opened the door with a jerk. He caught Kristie midknock.

Oblivious to his displeasure, she grinned at him. She had to look up to meet his glare, since she wasn't much more than five feet tall. "Good morning, Mr. Santana. Breakfast is ready. We have pancakes, eggs, muffins, fresh fruit, bacon and country ham."

"It's seven forty-five," Lucky grumbled.

Kristie cocked her head to one side, and her smile faded. "I'm so sorry."

Lucky began to nod. At least she had the good grace to apologize.

"Annie said you'd want to be up by seven-thirty, since you have a busy morning ahead of you, but I had my hands full in the kitchen and Stu was helping the Hendersons to their car. They had so much luggage, and as I'm sure you noticed, Mr. Henderson has a sprained wrist."

He hadn't noticed. Then again, he'd only passed the older couple in the downstairs hallway once, last night after his conversation with Murphy. His mind had been elsewhere at the time.

In truth, he was ready to start looking into the supposed murders that had Annie all wound up. And besides, he was hungry. "I'll be down in five minutes."

Kristie nodded, her smile widened to its usual brightness once again and she backed away. Her long dark hair was pulled back in a ponytail, and it flipped gently as she turned around. The woman looked like she'd just stepped out of a shampoo commercial, freshly scrubbed and squeaky clean.

He'd bet this woman and Annie were friends. Maybe that's why he was staying here instead of at a real hotel where they didn't wake you up at the crack of dawn unless you *personally* asked for a wake-up call.

The old house had been renovated so that each bedroom had its own bath, thank goodness. Lucky slammed his door and headed in the direction of the small bath that might've once been a closet—judging by the size. Shower, breakfast, Internet. And after he proved that Annie Lockhart was full of crap, he could brush her off with a clean conscience.

Training a bunch of green recruits and testing Murphy's newest toys was beginning to look damn good.

Annie spent Tuesday morning at the Mercerville location of Annie's Closet, delivering two hats, taking inventory and talking to the store manager about adding on new personnel for the busy holiday season. She didn't let on that her life had been turned upside down in the past few days. With any luck, no one would ever have to know.

She hadn't had disturbing dreams last night, but whatever was happening to her hadn't abated. As she looked around, she was all but assaulted with words and pictures that did not come from her own mind. If she concentrated, it all began to make sense. June, the manager, was preoccupied with her love life. A customer, someone Annie didn't know, was thinking of lifting a small purse and walking out with it, but she was being too closely watched so she didn't. She'd lift a different purse from a department store in Sevierville later this afternoon. Michelle, the newest employee, had dreams of owning a shop of her own one day, though she was really more interested in designing jewelry than hats and handbags. A woman picking up an order was thinking of her grocery list as she paid for her purchase. She was going to forget the milk.

Annie did her best to dismiss the intrusive thoughts of others and concentrate on small, ordinary things, like paying the bills and deciding what should go in the new window display. Eventually the nagging little voices faded, and then they stopped. Still, she was afraid they'd start again, so she took care of her business and very gratefully left the store—and all those jarring thoughts—behind. Home had never felt so good as it did when she closed the door behind her and experienced a moment of pure, total silence.

In the safety and silence of her own home, she had to ask herself the questions she most dreaded. What if this time the voices didn't stop? It was possible that Grams had been wrong, and, practice or not, the ability was here to stay. She was so certain that catching the killer would end this, but what if Lucky couldn't find the killer, or even worse, what if as soon as this murderer was caught, another round of violent dreams began?

What if the dreams stopped, but the newly rejuvenated psychic ability remained? Would she have to hide away for the rest of her life, keeping a distance between herself and others because she never knew when she might be assaulted by images and thoughts and secrets that were not her own?

As she had at the store, Annie buried herself in minute details that seemed to wipe away the thoughts she didn't need or want. She designed a new bag, organized the supplies that were crowding her out of her own great room, and balanced the checkbook. It was a pleasant and ordinary day. She really, really liked ordinary.

She expected Lucky to arrive at the cabin by two, and at 1:50 she heard his car pull into the driveway. As the car door slammed with excessive force, she held her breath and listened to the crisp steps on her front porch grow closer and louder.

He wasn't happy.

Annie waited for him to knock, and she wasn't surprised by the force of his knuckles on her front door. He would want explanations, *logical* explanations, and she didn't have any. She knew what she knew. There was no logic in it.

The confrontation was inevitable. She garnered her courage and opened the door to reveal an angry, tense, confused Lucky Santana.

He walked past her, shaking a notebook, which was now filled with loose sheets of paper that stuck out at all angles.

"How did you do it? How did you know this case stunk to high heaven?"

"Hello?" she said with a touch of sarcasm as she closed the door. "How are you? Lovely weather we're having."

He turned and glared at her, and looking into those vibrant eyes caused what felt like an electrical jolt to pass through her body.

"This isn't a social call," Lucky said with a decided lack of patience. "This is business. If you want chitchat, walk down the hill and visit with your perky friend Kristie."

He said "perky" as if it were an insult.

"There's no reason to make this unpleasant," Annie argued, even though there was nothing pleasant about this situation. Her knees wobbled a little, and that made her glad she was wearing a long, loose skirt. Maybe Lucky couldn't see her reaction. She crossed the room to take a chair before her knees gave out entirely. "Okay, everything about this is unpleasant. You know, I was half hoping that you'd come by and tell me I was wrong about everything. I'd be very happy to write this off as a nervous breakdown brought on by stress, but that's not the case, is it?" She lifted her head to look him in the eye.

"I don't have access to case files—not yet—but I did talk to an overly chatty deputy, and just checking the stories on the Internet and looking through newspapers at the library gave me a very clear picture of a piss-poor investigation and a lot of angry relatives who want answers they haven't gotten." A muscle in his taut jaw twitched. "There was no reason for Huff to murder his wife and then himself. None. From everything I've found, it looks like Jenna Huff was a dedicated, loving wife. Trey Huff was a simple enough guy who was well on his way to starting his own furniture refinishing business. He'd put a deposit down on a building, and had bought most of the supplies he needed to get started. The only explanation for a violent and unexpected mur-der/suicide is that Trey had a nervous breakdown, and that's extremely unlikely."

"I told you he didn't do it," she said. "Why do you sound so surprised?"

Again, that muscle in Lucky's jaw twitched. The man needed to relax in the worst way. "All of this hinges on a *dream*. That's not the way it works." He was desperate for logical answers. "I work for you, so you can tell me anything and everything without fear of reprisal. Did you talk to someone who saw something they shouldn't? Do you know who did this, and you're afraid to tell me or anyone else how you know? Give me something I can work with, Annie. Tell me the truth."

"I've never told you anything but the truth."

Frustration shone through, even though he tried to appear calm and reasonable. "At the very least, let me take this to the sheriff."

Ignoring the lurch of her heart, Annie gestured for Lucky to sit down, and after a moment of hesitation he did. He tossed his notebook to an end table and gripped the bridge of his nose between two fingers as he closed his eyes and reached for the calm and patience he wished to possess. Neither came naturally to him.

He wasn't going to like what she had to say, but he needed to hear it.

"Five years ago, when I lived in Nashville, I had a dream about a murder. The dream was very much like the ones I've been having lately. Violent, vivid, all too real." She told him the details, as quickly and painlessly as she could. She spared him the gory details of the dreams themselves. "A woman was killed, supposedly during a break-in at her apartment. It was her boyfriend. Thanks to the dreams I knew it was him, without a

single doubt, so I went to the police. They didn't believe
me, of course, but when it turned out I was right about
some of the details…" She shrugged her shoulders,
trying to make it appear that the details didn't matter,
when in fact they mattered very much. "I don't want to
relive that time, not even to tell you how they treated me,
how I was questioned, what it felt like to believe that I
was going to end up in prison for a crime I didn't
commit because I tried to help. I can't go to the sheriff
with this, and neither can you. They won't believe either
of us."

Lucky took a deep breath. He wanted to get out of
here so badly. She hated that. They gotten off to a rocky
start, but she did like him, and there was that vision of
what was to be. What *might* be.

For a moment she had a clear and uncluttered
glimpse into Lucky's complicated mind. He wasn't
thinking of a grocery list, or his love life, or shoplift-
ing. Instead he was thinking about her and this case and
how much he didn't want to believe her. A part of him
did believe, though, and that scared him a little. She
didn't want him to be scared of her.

She also didn't want to spend her life seeing into
other people's hearts and minds. Sitting there, Annie did
her best to shut Lucky out. She did everything she could
to quiet the ability that had brought him here. After a
moment, it began to work. She *could* shut down her
abilities. She *could* put up a shield that would keep
Lucky, and everyone else, out of her head. She erected
that shield now, basically separating herself from him
and everyone else. A moment of calm descended, and

she breathed a sigh of relief, even though she had no idea how long the shield would last.

If she wanted this thing to go away altogether, she had to help Lucky find the man who had murdered Trey and Jenna Huff.

"I understand your reasoning, but I still think we should take what we have to the sheriff," Lucky said after a long moment of silence. "Without the case files I can't—"

"No!" Annie came up out of her chair. "Didn't you hear a word I said about what happened in Nashville? Do I have to go into detail to make you understand? Fine. I lost the man I loved, my friends, my job, my *life*. I won't go through that again. I hired you, Mr. Santana. You work for me, and I will not allow you to take what I've told you to the sheriff or anyone else. Is that clear?" When he didn't respond she asked again, more loudly. "Is that clear?"

"Yes, ma'am," Lucky answered sarcastically. "I'll just sit on the knowledge that a man has gotten away with murder."

Drained and frustrated, Annie sat once again. "We have to stop him, I know that. I'm not suggesting that we do nothing. With what I've told you, you should be able to find out who the killer is and collect some hard evidence and then take *that* to the sheriff."

"You want me to work the case backward."

"Sure. Why not?"

Lucky leaned back in his chair and thrust out long legs. He appeared to relax, but in truth he was still wound tight. It took no unnatural gift to see that fact. Was he always so tense?

"It's going to take time."

Annie closed her eyes. She had some money saved, and if she held off on opening the third store she could afford to keep Lucky on the payroll for a week or two. Would that be enough? The Benning Agency didn't come cheap, and while she had money, she was far from independently wealthy.

"Do it," she finally said. What choice did she have?

She heard the rustle of papers, and opened her eyes to see Lucky spreading his notes across the table where they'd worked last night. Relief spread through her, warming her body from head to toe. This time she wasn't alone. This time she had Lucky Santana to help her.

"Thank you," she whispered.

"You're welcome," he responded dryly, without pausing in his work. When he had the papers arranged in a manner that suited him, he turned to her. "I'm not saying that I don't believe you, but I still think it's possible that there's a reasonable explanation for the way you figured this out. You read the articles in the newspaper, you saw the relatives on television, you…you put two and two together, and the pieces came together in your dreams."

"If that's what you have to believe in order to do what has to be done, then do it. I don't care."

"Just one thing," he said too casually. "Who told you about Sadie? Not that there's anything to tell, mind you, but she is my old partner, and there was a time when…well, someone might've thought that I… So, who told you about Sadie? Cal? Dante?"

"You told me," Annie answered in a lowered voice.

Lucky glared at her. He was, at this moment, a little angry, very puzzled and more than a little determined. Determination on a man like Lucky Santana was very appealing. There weren't very many men like this one in the world, and wasn't that a pity.

"Fine," he snapped. "If you're really psychic, then get me something I can use. How about the killer's address?"

The rain started to fall while Annie studied his notes and—on occasion—touched them. Lucky kept his eyes on her face. He saw her anxiety, her indecision and her dread at the job she had before her.

He'd asked her to try to see more, in order to give him something to work with. She didn't want to, but she'd consented. They had come to a compromise. He wouldn't mention her name to the sheriff; she would try to bring on the visions that she obviously didn't want.

Her reluctance made him think maybe…just maybe…she had an ability he didn't understand. Then again, she might just be a very good actress.

He didn't think she was acting.

The most logical explanation for Annie's suppositions about the Huffs' deaths was the one he'd put to her earlier; she'd put two and two together in the back of her mind and came up with dreams that seemed real. She didn't believe that explanation, but the brain was a complicated machine, and anything was possible. Well, almost anything.

For the moment, he was stuck here. Not because Cal had sent him here, not because Annie had hired him. He felt responsible for Annie Lockhart. She needed him, and he couldn't turn his back on her. That was his downfall. Always.

She even looked like a kook. Today she didn't wear low-rise jeans and a snug T-shirt, but instead had dressed in a long, full bluish-greenish skirt, a white blouse with a touch of ruffles and sandals. The toenails were still pink, but the yellow toe ring had been replaced with plain silver. Her short blond hair looked purposely mussed— he supposed it was meant to be trendy—and long silver earrings dangled almost to her shoulders. Everything about her screamed damsel in distress. His weakness.

Even when she attempted to be tough, as she had when she'd put him in his place a couple of hours ago, there was a vulnerability in Annie Lockhart that appealed to his hero-complex. Save the girl, allow her to get as close as was wise and then walk away before she got too close. Wasn't that the way it always worked? For the past few years, anyway. At least he had learned to walk away before everything went to hell.

"He watched them," Annie said softly, her fingertips tailing across a sheet of paper. "For a long time, he watched. He was drawn to their happiness because he has none of his own."

"That's fine," Lucky said in a reassuring voice. "Good. What else do you see? Can you look beyond his mind to what was going on around him? What does he look like? Did the Huffs know him? Did they trust him?" How else could the killer have gotten so close?

"He watched from a distance at first, and then he moved closer." She shivered, almost uncontrollably.

"They knew him. They weren't afraid until it was too late." She closed her eyes and swayed slightly, and Lucky immediately placed his arm around her and drew her away from the table.

"That's enough for now," he said. "I don't want you passing out on me." He lowered her into her chair, and there she leaned her head back and took a deep, cleansing breath. He watched her closely, as the color returned to her face.

"We'll do this in stages," he said. "I don't want you trying to do too much at once." Whether her ability was real or imagined, she did exhaust herself when she reached for visions.

A timid smile transformed her face. "You're very protective."

"It's my job."

"But this isn't a normal job, is it?" she asked.

"Not even close. In Nashville, you knew who the killer was. This time, things seem to be less clear. Why?"

Annie shuddered. "Back then I saw it all, as if I were a fly on the wall. Now I seem to be watching through the killer's eyes. I can't *see* him." She closed her eyes. "It's very frustrating."

Lucky tried to ignore Annie's responses while he made work of straightening his notes. He still hadn't decided how he was going to tell Cal it was possible the kook was legit. At the very least, she'd pointed him toward a case that didn't make any sense, and he couldn't walk away.

As for how… He was still putting his money on some hard-to-explain function of the brain. Some people were good at math. Annie was just good with disjointed puzzles. Whatever the reason, with luck she'd soon lead him right to the killer. If not, he'd find evidence on his own. He'd gather evidence, work the case backward, invent some legitimate reasoning for the investigation and put the bad guy behind bars. No one would ever have to know that Annie had led him to the killer.

But he'd know. How would he ever approach any other investigation without wondering what she was thinking? What she might know that he couldn't see? The fact that one person might actually be able to glimpse into the mind of another was intriguing. Impossible, *improbable*, but intriguing. If nothing else, her brain was great at working puzzles. Maybe he could use Annie in the future, when a mystery presented itself. It wasn't necessary that anyone else know, but how could something so powerful and useful be ignored?

There was only one other possible explanation for her knowledge. She was somehow involved in the murders. He immediately dismissed that idea. Annie Lockhart annoyed him to no end. She was fascinating and maddening. And she was no killer.

Again he told himself that she was not his type, but now and then when he looked at her she was beyond pretty. Not gorgeous, not eye-popping, but beautiful all the same. Of course, she also looked like she might walk out the door at any time and hug a tree, or pick wildflowers and start to dance and skip with the animals.

It was in his basic makeup to wonder what she'd look

like naked, and he pondered the possibilities as he fiddled needlessly with his notes. Leggy, curvy, soft, delicate. She was all those things, he could see that well enough even when she was dressed.

But what would she taste like? Did she kiss with the trepidation he so often saw from her, or with the ferocity she displayed when she lost her temper? He was guessing a bit of both. Annie was a complicated woman, and every man alive knew that complicated women were nothing but trouble. Brainless bimbos were easier to handle. A man never had to wonder what she was thinking, because she usually wasn't.

Complicated or not, he did wonder—again—what Annie Lockhart would taste like. It was in his nature to wonder about such things, and a man who fought his own nature was fighting a losing battle.

He didn't hear her move, but suddenly there was a soft, warm hand on his back and a gentle voice said, "There's only one way to find out."

They skipped past all the steps most men and women covered before getting to the kissing part. No flirty smiles, no awkward date, no touch of one hand to another, no not-so-accidental brushes of one body against another. No, she and Lucky went straight to the mouth-to-mouth stage.

He turned to face her, she went up on her toes and their mouths came together.

His thoughts had drawn her to him, in an undeniable way. Unlike the jarring and unwanted images she'd been suffering of late, Lucky's reflections on how she might taste had seemed almost like her own thoughts. They were mingled with her own, not intrusive and strange. In the shop, the thoughts of others had come to her in a jarring and unpleasant way, almost as if they were shouting into her brain, and reaching for a killer had been draining and unpleasant. Lucky's contemplations were mellow and easy. They were pleasant, and she needed that right now.

It had been a long time since she'd kissed a man. Years, in fact. And still, kissing Lucky seemed very natural. It was a kiss she felt throughout her body. Warm, arousing, comforting, dangerous—it was everything a kiss could and should be.

She liked it.

Rain pattered on the roof and the windows, isolating them. Outside this cabin the world was wet and windy, but inside there was safety and warmth.

For a few precious seconds Annie forgot all the unpleasantness that had brought them together, and just enjoyed the kiss. She leaned into Lucky; one of his arms encircled her, but not too tightly. He tasted of warmth and masculinity and security, and she loved the feel of his solid body against hers. It had been too long....

How did she taste to him? Even though they were touching, kissing, joined in a very primal way, she didn't know. That was very nice. Something in her life should be normal, even if it was just a kiss.

And then without warning something of Lucky did speak to her, and it was so real she had no doubts about her interpretation. *Save the girl, take what you can get, walk away before she gets too close*. It wasn't a plan, exactly. He wasn't even aware the thought had passed through his mind—he was totally engrossed in the kiss, and he wasn't thinking of anything else.

But what she saw, what she felt…it was the way he lived his life. At least she'd know what to expect, if this went any further than a kiss. She couldn't let herself love Lucky Santana, not ever, because he didn't know how to love her or any other woman.

She barely knew the man, so the word *love* shouldn't even come into play. But there it was, dancing just out of reach. Lucky didn't know what love was. To him the word was related to trust, or sex, or commitment. He'd never combined the first two, and he'd never truly experienced the third.

Did she know what love was? In the past she'd thought so, but it had ended badly…. She wasn't so sure now.

She ended the kiss, and placed one palm against Lucky's solid, warm chest. He would like to appear unaffected, but his heart beat too fast, just as hers did. "I needed that," she said softly.

Lucky would never admit to as much, but he'd needed the kiss, too. And he'd liked it. As she returned to her chair he said, "You are the oddest woman I've ever met."

Normally she wouldn't take that comment as a compliment, but there was some flattery intended, she knew. "Thank you," she said as she sank back into the chair and closed her eyes, not to relive the pain of reaching for a killer, but to commit to memory the beauty and wonder of a first kiss.

Chapter 4

Lucky's usual professional attire—a good suit and a crisp white dress shirt—made him stand out like a sore thumb in Mercerville. It was a casual little town, filled with laid-back tourists and homey citizens. Fortunately, he'd packed more casual clothes, and when he headed into town on Wednesday morning he was wearing khaki pants and a dark green golf shirt. Maybe today people wouldn't stare, as they had yesterday when he'd visited the small but well-stocked library.

Downtown Mercerville gave him the creeps. With those homey citizens who all seemed to know one another well—perhaps too well—and the too-quaint-to-be-real appearance of the downtown area, he pretty much expected blank-eyed children or toothless men bearing pitchforks to bear down on him at any moment.

He was very much a city boy. He enjoyed the quiet solitude of the house he'd bought three years ago, but downtown Nashville wasn't all that far away, and he spent more than his share of time there.

This…this was practically archaic.

Annie's Closet was located in a prime downtown Mercerville spot, on a corner that looked to be *the* intersection. The other three corners were occupied by a pharmacy, a quaint café, and what looked to be an upscale restaurant. The rest of the area was populated with other small shops that would attract tourists. Antiques, souvenirs, T-shirts, fudge. An entire business devoted to making and selling *fudge*.

As he passed by Annie's Closet, he saw some of Annie's personality in the window display. Even though she had several employees, she'd probably arranged it herself. The contents of the display were colorful, bright and decidedly odd. Scarves were draped this way and that, and women's purses and hats were arranged in a haphazard way that was somehow not at all haphazard. Annie was apparently fond of sparkly stuff, since there was plenty of it on display.

The woman who'd hired him kissed the same way she did everything else. With abandon. It had been a long time since any woman had been able to surprise him, but yesterday Annie had done just that.

Not that there was necessarily anything paranormal about her knowledge that he'd been thinking of kissing her. He was a man; she was a woman. It was absolutely natural that he might be thinking about what she might taste like.

Well, now he knew. She tasted damn good. From here on out their relationship would be entirely professional.

Three short blocks down the road, the courthouse, library and post office comprised the official presence of Mercerville. The sheriff's office was located on the second floor of the courthouse—which looked as if it had been standing since the nineteenth century. It was architecturally impressive, and as creepy as the rest of the small town.

His mother had come from a small town much like this one. It had been located in Mississippi, not Tennessee, but that didn't matter much. In places like this one everyone knew everyone else's business, and once you were out of the loop, you were completely out. Small-town people could be unforgiving and cruel, in the worst sort of way.

No wonder Mercerville gave him the creeps.

Lucky walked from his parking space just outside Annie's Closet to the courthouse, passing tourists and locals on the way. They still studied him as he passed, but not as fiercely as they had yesterday. Maybe if he stepped into that shop that had garden flags and rakes in the window and purchased a pair of overalls and a wide-brimmed straw hat…

He almost smiled. That would be the day.

In the courthouse, Lucky bypassed the ancient elevator and bounded up the stairs to the second floor. Annie insisted that he not tell the sheriff that her dreams had brought him here, but that didn't mean he couldn't let the man and his people know that the Huffs' deaths were currently under investigation by the Benning Agency.

* * *

Annie found herself busy in the kitchen again. It was nice to have someone to cook for, and Lucky looked as if he could use the food. He probably ate in restaurants all the time, and lived on cereal and frozen meals when he did eat at home. The man definitely needed some domestic care and attention.

Once again last night she'd managed to sleep without disturbing dreams, a fact that was responsible for her chipper mood. If she'd dreamed at all she'd already forgotten the details, which was wonderful. Normal and average and absolutely wonderful.

She recognized Lucky's knock, and all but bounded to the door to answer. He looked decidedly sour.

"Don't you ever comb your hair?" he asked as he stepped into her home. "Or wear shoes?"

She turned her back on him and headed for the kitchen, a soft smile on her face. "Do you always dress like my father?"

"Cute," he mumbled beneath his breath. He followed her to the kitchen and made himself comfortable against the doorjamb, leaning there and watching her as she returned to her domestic chores. For a few minutes he was silent. He was watching her; she knew without turning about to face him.

"Your Sheriff Buhl is not a cooperative man."

Her heart skipped a beat at his mention of the sheriff, even though he had promised that her name would not be mentioned in relation to the investigation. "Did you think he would be?" She cast a glance in Lucky's direction.

"I thought he might at least talk to me," Lucky

grumbled. "Instead he warned me to steer clear of the Huff case, which he declared closed without question."

"I don't think he's a bad sheriff," Annie said as she stirred the chicken and dumplings. "He's just tired. A little lazy. It causes him to take shortcuts when they present themselves. Besides, you're a stranger here. Sheriff Buhl doesn't trust strangers."

"Is this another psychic observation?" Lucky asked caustically.

"No. I've lived here for over four years. People talk."

Even in what he considered casual wear, he looked stiff and overly conservative. Annie couldn't help but wonder, as she set the table and poured two tall glasses of sweet iced tea, what he'd look like in worn jeans that would hug those strong thighs, a black T-shirt that would mold to his muscles and maybe well-used work boots that would clomp across her wooden floor with authority. If his hair grew a little long, and he didn't shave for a day or two... She glanced at him as she wondered. With those eyes, he'd look dangerous no matter what he wore. Besides, he likely didn't own a pair of worn jeans or a too-small black T-shirt.

Too bad.

Didn't the woman ever wear a bra? It wasn't that she actually needed one. Annie was firm and not exactly huge in the breast department. Still, there was something about the knowledge that she wasn't wearing one that crept into his brain and wouldn't go away.

He really, really hoped she wasn't able to read his mind.

"So, what do you think?" She plopped down into the

chair that he thought of as hers, the old yellow armchair she usually sat in, tucking one bare foot beneath her. Tonight's jeans were even more worn than the first pair he'd seen her wear. There was even a small, frayed hole high on the right leg that offered a tiny glimpse of skin.

Lucky turned his mind as completely as possible away from Annie, her breasts and her bed, and concentrated on the case. "There's not much more I can do here, if the sheriff won't cooperate."

Her small smile died, and her eyes flashed. Not with anger, but with fear. "You're leaving?"

"In the morning," he said calmly. "But I'm not giving up. I have a friend who's a sheriff in Alabama." Well, technically Truman was married to a friend, but that was close enough to the truth. "I'll have him make some official inquiries. Maybe he can get Sheriff Buhl to let loose of the official case file."

"And if he doesn't?"

"Then I'll think of something else." He intended to sound reassuring, but to Annie it probably sounded more like a cop-out. "Trust me," he added.

A sly, uncertain smile crept across her face. "When a man says those words, it's usually time to take cover."

"Not this time," he said, and her smile disappeared.

"I don't know how you did it," he continued. "I'm not yet ready to say that I believe in psychic ability or prophetic dreams or any of that woo woo, but you have stumbled into something. The case is wrong. I won't walk away from it."

"Thank you," she said, less than enthusiastically.

There was no need to go over notes again tonight,

and he didn't want to ask her to try to see anything new about the killer. It had drained her last time, putting her very firmly in the damsel-in-distress category. He had all he needed, for now.

Annie looked good, sitting in a relaxed pose, staring at him with those big blue eyes. Like it or not, she was tempting. He really didn't have time for *tempting*.

Lucky said good night. There was no kiss this time; he didn't even shake her hand. He thanked Annie for supper, and told her he'd call if…when…he found anything. She remained in her chair and offered a poor attempt at a smile.

On her front porch, with the door closed behind him, Lucky stopped and looked out over the mountains. They were everything mountains should be. Majestic and awe inspiring. While he stood there, he took his phone from the pocket of his khakis and flipped it open, keying in a familiar number from memory.

Cal answered with a gruff hello.

"Did anyone but you talk to Annie Lockhart?" he asked without preamble.

"No."

"You're sure?"

"Yes. What's this about? Murphy said you were going to stay and look into the kook's case for a couple of days. Are you that desperate not to train the new guys? They're not all that bad…."

"Did you tell Lockhart anything personal about me? Anything at all that she shouldn't know?"

There was a long moment of silence before Cal answered. "No. Man, don't tell me she's pulling some fortune-teller con on you. They can do that, you know. If anyone's too smart to fall for that crap, it's you."

"No con," Lucky replied. "I think maybe she's the real deal."

After another long moment of silence, Cal began to laugh. "Very funny. Ha-ha. You had me going there, for a minute. When are you headed back?"

"In the morning," Lucky said as he walked down the front steps of Annie's cabin and headed for his car. He didn't bother to tell Cal that the job wasn't over yet. That could wait until he was looking the man in the eye. Somebody had told Annie about Sadie. But who?

Lucky wasn't going to be here long enough to follow through with any of the personal images she caught from him on occasion. Annie knew she should be relieved, but instead she felt cheated and deeply disappointed.

She dressed for bed—in blue-and-white-striped pajama bottoms and a cropped white shirt—and checked to make sure all her doors and windows were locked. She knew they were, and still she tested each one. The front door, which Lucky had locked as he'd left. The kitchen door, which opened onto the deck that ran the length of the back of the cabin. The windows throughout the cabin. The sliding glass door in her bedroom that also opened onto the deck.

Only when that was done did she slip beneath the covers. Over her head, the fan whirred, slow and silent and unobstructed. So much for her vision of Lucky in this bed, with that fan rotating beyond his scarred shoulder. Maybe that hadn't been a vision after all, but was nothing more than wishful thinking.

She really had been too long without a man.

It wasn't as if she'd never thought about finding that right man, falling in love, getting married and having two or three kids. That was the all-American dream, right?

But not only did she have her parents' disaster of a marriage to consider, she also had her experience in Nashville. She'd thought Seth was the right man. They'd dated a few times, and she'd quickly fallen in love. Seth had been sweet and funny and attentive. He'd been wonderfully normal, a rock-solid kind of guy. They'd talked about getting married. She'd been given to daydreams about how many children they might have, and where they'd buy their first house. And then Seth had learned that she was not what he'd thought her to be, and it had all gone away.

During that very bad time in Nashville, most of the people she talked to thought she was nuts. Not Seth. She'd convinced him of what she could do—just as she'd tried to convince Lucky. She'd convinced him, and he'd been terrified of her. Just like that, with a snap of her fingers, it was over. That was when she'd learned that love was very, very fragile.

And so was she. The end of that relationship had hurt, more than anything else. More than the possibility of going to jail. More than the possibility of being a freak forever. Love—here one minute and gone the next, with no trace but a broken heart to prove it ever existed.

Maybe that was one of the attractive attributes Lucky presented. He might want her, but he would never love her.

It was a pretty, cloudless night, with a bite of fall in the air. He stood in the shadow of the wood far from the road and lifted his binoculars, holding his breath until he caught sight of the couple he sought. They were so beautiful, so much in love. A smile spread across his face as he watched. The window, which overlooked the mountain, was uncovered. There was no reason to cover a window that looked out over wilderness. Who would imagine that someone would stand here in the night and watch?

Night was best for watching. Bright lights inside the house illuminated the couple in the window as if they were on display just for him. It was like watching TV, but this show was for him alone.

Beneath his feet, fallen leaves cushioned the hard ground. He might be more comfortable if he sat, but not only were the leaves still slightly damp from recent rain, if he sat he wouldn't be able to see, and he needed to see. So he continued to stand, his view unobstructed.

Behind him, something small scurried. He paid it no mind. The animal that made the noise was too small to be of concern to him, and if something else came along, well, he was armed.

But no larger critters came along, and eventually even the smaller ones grew still and quiet. That was good. He didn't want to be distracted.

His smile faded when the happy couple stepped away from the window, even though he was almost certain they would be back. The wide, tall window that

afforded him such a great view was on the back side of
the one-story house, and that was one of their favorite
rooms. It was a sitting room, or a private study, and that
was where they retired in the evening when all their
work was done. Last night they had been in that room
for two hours, before turning out the lights. They'd
been together all night, of course. They were very much
in love, so they enjoyed being together.

After puttering about the room, straightening a few
things and writing something at her desk, the woman
he watched settled into her favorite chair with a book.
He liked the way she tucked her feet beneath her, the
way her hair swayed to one side. She only read for a few
minutes before her husband joined her. He placed a
hand on her shoulder, and in the woods the man with
binoculars could almost feel that touch. It made him
shudder, but in a good way, as if he'd been touched, too.
The woman in the comfortable chair looked over her
shoulder and smiled, and slowly closed her book. The
man said something, something that made her laugh and
then reach for the light to turn it off.

Again, the man in the woods held his breath, but the
light didn't come back on. His grip on the binoculars
grew tighter. They were making love in their bedroom,
he knew it. Their bedroom had a small, unacceptable
window, which was always covered and faced another
house. Even if he could see through that window, there
was no way he could watch unobserved.

He could not watch what was happening, so he
allowed his imagination to run wild. In his mind he saw
them undress one another, fall into a large, soft bed and

make love. Easy at first, and then not so easy. Perhaps she would scream. If he strained, would he be able to hear? No, he was too far away. His imagination would have to suffice, for now.

When they were finished they would lie together and whisper in the dark. They would declare their love and laugh, and they would share secrets they wanted no one else to hear. Maybe they would make love again.

He wanted to see; he wanted to hear those whispers.

He had to get closer.

Lucky should've been asleep hours ago, but his mind was spinning and every muscle in his body was tense. Maybe he should just get in his car and drive home tonight. Surely he'd be able to sleep in his own bed, even if only for a couple of hours. There really wasn't any reason to wait around here until morning, especially if he couldn't sleep.

It was that damned woman, preying on his mind. Cal had called her a kook from day one, and that wasn't far from wrong. It wasn't just the psychic thing that made Annie different. Everything about her was odd. She apparently disliked shoes, her clothes were anything but conventional and her hair always seemed just enough mussed that he assumed it was a style and not a severe case of bed-head. She wore toe rings, and while he had not yet found a tattoo, he would still bet money she had one. Probably on her ass. Chicks went for that sort of thing. She looked like a twenty-first-century blond gypsy.

Annie was pretty, and appealing in an unexpected

sort of way, and she definitely knew how to kiss. She just wasn't his type. Dante would probably appreciate her avant-garde style, and they could compare tattoos all night long. Murphy would enjoy her laugh—and it was really a pretty good laugh, even if he hadn't heard much of it. Sadie would like her. At first glance they didn't have anything in common, but beneath the skin where it really counted…they were just enough alike to become friends.

He'd never before dated a woman that Sadie liked, much less one that might turn into a friend. Not that he was going to date Annie, or take her to Sadie's for Thanksgiving, or kiss her again. Ever. He'd finish up the investigation and call her with a report—if he had anything to report. Maybe once he got away from here he'd see the case in a different light. Maybe the murder/suicide was exactly what it seemed, inconsistencies and all.

He knew what really drew him to Annie Lockhart, and it had nothing to do with the Huffs and their tragic deaths. Annie spoke to his weakness. His damned Achilles' heel. She needed him. She was scared and she'd turned to him for help. No one else. Just him. One of these days he was going to have to get rid of his damsel-in-distress fixation. He was never going to get married again, but that didn't mean he couldn't have some sort of normal relationship with a person of the opposite sex, preferably someone who didn't need a knight in shining armor.

If only he had a clue what normal was….

When his cell phone rang, he glanced at the bedside clock. When the phone rang at three in the morning, there had to be an emergency. With any luck it would be an emergency that necessitated a quick drive away from Mercerville, Tennessee.

But he recognized the number on the caller ID. Annie Lockhart. This couldn't be good.

"What?" he answered brusquely, expecting a vivid account of yet another dream.

For a moment all he heard was frantic, heavy breathing.

"Talk to me, Annie." Must've been one helluva dream. "Come on. Calm down and tell me what happened."

From the other end of the line there was a gasp, a sob, and then—finally—a very softly spoken and frightened "Help me, Lucky. He's…he's here."

Chapter 5

Annie's entire body shook. Some of the shaking was caused by the cool night air, since she sat on the front porch with her eyes on the drive and she wore nothing more than her summery pajamas. Most of the shaking was caused by the remnants of the dream that had awakened her to the sound of a scream. Her own scream.

One thought kept her from screaming again. Lucky was coming. Everything would be all right when he got here. She clasped the portable phone in her hand, even though Lucky was no longer on the other end of the line. Somewhere along the way the signal had died. Damn cell phones. There were too many pockets up here where the reception was lousy.

Annie dropped the phone to the porch, buried her face in her hands and took a deep breath of the night air. It was just cold enough to bite at her lungs, and she liked the feeling. That cold bite reminded her that she was alive, that this was real life, not a dream.

She heard Lucky's car before she saw it. The engine was working at full power. He was racing up the hill to get to her; he was coming as fast as he could. That was what he was, who he thought himself to be, anyway. A rescuer. A defender. A man who carried the weight of the world on his shoulders. The weight of her world, at least for tonight.

At the moment, he was the only person in the world she could trust with her secret. He might not believe her, at least not entirely, but he hadn't pulled away from her in fear, either. He hadn't accused her of having something to do with the murders she knew too much about, or of making it all up in order to garner some sick sort of attention. If only she had known him, or someone like him, five years ago…

When would he get here? The seconds went by too slowly. She had to tell him everything about the latest nightmare before she forgot the details—as if she could ever forget.

Lucky's car screeched to a stop, and he threw open the door. He didn't even take the time to close it as he ran toward her, gun in hand. Where had he gotten a gun? And what on earth was that going to do against a dream?

No, not a dream. A nightmare. A vision.

He ran onto the porch, feet bare, no shirt, wrinkled trousers clearly scooped from the floor as he ran from the bed-and-breakfast. She liked that—that in spite of his usually pristine appearance, he was human enough to throw his clothes onto the floor at the end of the day. She concentrated on the wrinkles for a moment, losing herself in the concrete reality of the details.

There was just enough light from the moon and the cabin behind her to allow her to see the small scar on his shoulder. It was just as she'd seen in her vision; small and thin and oddly crooked, and so old he rarely thought about it anymore.

After glancing around the porch and the front yard, Lucky dropped down to his haunches and in a lowered voice asked, "Where is he?"

"He's here," Annie said, as she had when she'd heard Lucky's voice over the telephone. She didn't mean for her voice to shake, but it did.

Lucky rose slowly. "In the house?"

Annie shook her head. "No, not *here* here. He's in Mercerville, and he's already chosen another couple to watch and to…to kill."

Lucky stood very still for a long, silent moment. "You said he was here."

"He is. He's…"

"No, you said *here!*"

It was a good thing she didn't have any close neighbors. That incensed shout echoed through the night.

"I tried to explain, but you hung up on me," she said, fighting her way to her feet—shaking knees be damned.

"I didn't hang up on you," Lucky said tersely. "I lost the signal running down the stairs, and I didn't want to take the time to dial your number, since I thought the bad guy was *here*."

Annie turned and opened her front door. "There's no reason to be testy."

Lucky followed her inside. "There's every reason in the world to be testy, dammit."

"I panicked," she explained.

"No kidding."

"I'm sorry I called you," she said. Disappointment welled up inside her. So much for her personal champion. So much for finally having someone she could trust and confide in and lean on. "You can leave now."

"I don't think so." Lucky caught her arm, spun her around and kissed her. Unlike the last kiss, he was prepared. Heavens, was he prepared. He kissed her very, very thoroughly, and she allowed herself to enjoy for a moment, and then to kiss him back. The dream faded away; it was pushed to the back of her mind while he kissed her.

It was such a wonderful kiss, it didn't take her long to become very aware of the fact that she was in light-weight pajamas and he was wearing nothing but a pair of wrinkled khakis. A word from her, a single word, and they could—and would—end up in her bed. No nightmares would dare to come while Lucky was in the bed with her. And if they did, she'd have someone to hold on to to make the fear go away. This was reality. Wonderful, concrete, stunningly beautiful reality.

He caught her lower lip between his teeth, and she teased him with the tip of her tongue. It was…nice. One of his very large hands settled at her back, possessive and warm and comforting. That hand fell to her hip, where it rested as if it belonged there. And all the while, he kissed her. The horror of the dream faded.

Eventually Lucky pulled away. His movements were slow and reluctant, but he did end the kiss and take a single step back. "You scared the crap out of me," he said, his voice gruffly accusing.

"Sorry," she whispered. A part of her wanted to take his hand and lead him down the hallway to her bed, where they would chase away the bad memories with good ones. She was tempted, but scared as she was she knew that fear and loneliness were poor reasons for taking such a momentous step.

Some people could have sex just for companionship, physical pleasure and fun. She couldn't. Sex was as much of the heart and soul as the body, at least for her. Why did she have to be old-fashioned in this one way? Why couldn't she take Lucky's hand and smile widely and promise him everything he'd ever wanted from a woman? He'd never cared about capturing any woman's heart, after all. His conquests were all about the body, nothing more.

He placed one of his hands on her cheek. It was warm and strong, and it made her wish she could be casual, that she could have a physical relationship without thinking about what tomorrow might bring.

"You're still scared." Lucky's thumb rocked across her jaw as he made this observation.

"Yeah."

"You had another dream that's more than a dream."

She nodded.

Lucky sighed and dropped his hand. "Tell me all about it."

* * *

Lucky wouldn't admit to Annie, or anyone else, how scared he'd been when he'd thought the man who'd murdered the Huffs was in her house. He hadn't seen the crime-scene photos or read the autopsy reports, but the newspapers had been graphic enough for him to construct a mental picture. If her dreams were so real, no wonder they terrified her.

Annie's dream, the one that had scared her into calling him in the middle of the night, had convinced her that the man who'd murdered the Huffs and made it look like a murder/suicide was still in Mercerville, and he planned to kill again. Apparently he had already chosen his next targets, and had begun to watch.

The very idea gave him the creeps. As Lucky sat in the living room in the near dark and watched Annie sleep on a short sofa, he had to at least ponder the possibility that there was some truth to Annie's suppositions. The Huff case definitely stank, and the scenario Annie had presented to him was at the very least plausible. He still didn't believe in psychic ability, not entirely, but how could he dismiss Annie's dreams if there was even the smallest possibility she was right?

Even after she'd calmed down and he'd promised that he'd stay for the night, Annie had refused to return to her bed, opting for the couch instead. He didn't mind. Here he could watch her, make sure she remained safe. At this point sleep was impossible for him, and it wouldn't be the first night he'd passed without sleep. For now he would watch her and keep her safe. He could return to his rented room in the morning and fetch decent clothing. And shoes.

As the sun was rising, he dozed in the chair. The cabin was quiet, Annie slept deeply and he was exhausted. Now and then he woke and glanced around the room, and after convincing himself that all was well he quickly returned to dreamland.

Fortunately for him, his dreamland was much nicer than Annie's. It was disjointed, in that way dreams can be, and Annie was there. In his dreams she was naked, more often than not.

It was midmorning before he woke completely, and the waking came to the tune of a resounding knock on Annie's front door. He came out of the chair slowly, muscles that were not accustomed to sleeping in chairs creaking slightly. There had been a time when he could sleep anywhere and not suffer adverse effects, but at thirty-six his body had become more demanding. He liked sleeping in a bed.

Annie was headed for the door, still wearing her pajamas, her short blond hair going this way and that. She ran a distracted hand through the spiky strands before opening the door, for all the good it did.

She opened the door to reveal the sheriff who, judging by the expression on his face, was none too happy.

Sheriff Buhl was pushing fifty. He was thin and ropey, and on the few occasions Lucky had seen him, he'd always looked royally pissed. He was pissed now. The annoyed sheriff stepped into the cabin, looking right past Annie to a sleep-rumpled and half-dressed Lucky. He took in Annie's pajamas and disheveled state, and Lucky's state of dress, and made his own conclusions.

"I got a phone call this morning," the man snapped,

"from a sheriff in Alabama. He asked me if I'd do him the personal favor of sharing my files on the Huff case."

It was then that Lucky noticed the pitifully thin file the sheriff held in one hand. The edge of that file tapped nervously against one khaki-clad leg.

"I was reluctant to share," Sheriff Buhl said. "But Sheriff McCain tells me you were once a damn fine cop, and he pointed out more than once that I don't have anything to lose by letting you look over the file." With a flick of the sheriff's bony wrist, the file in question took a short sail onto the couch where Annie had slept for the past few hours.

Lucky had a few questions—like what else Truman had said to make Sheriff Buhl share, and how the sheriff had found him here at Annie's cabin. Perky Kristie was likely guilty where that second question was concerned. She knew if he wasn't in his room, he was probably here. "Thank you," he said. "I'll let you know what I find."

"Damn straight you will," the sheriff grumbled. "Trey Huff was a good fella, and I would love any excuse to believe that he didn't do this terrible thing."

Lucky nodded.

"I don't think you're gonna find anything, though," the aggravated man continued. His eyes flitted, again, from Annie to Lucky. "I don't think a man who works for an outfit like the Benning Agency investigates cases like this on a whim. Who hired you? Her?" He sounded confused, and why not? Annie hadn't even known the Huffs.

"I'm afraid I can't reveal my client's name."

"Don't look at me," Annie said, lying well. "Lucky came into the store yesterday asking questions about the

Huffs. I didn't know them so I couldn't help, but we hit it off right away, and…well, you know how it is."

"Not really," Sheriff Buhl mumbled. As he turned to exit he added, "I'll tell Jerry you said hello."

"Yes, please do," Annie said brightly just before the front door slammed shut.

Annie continued to face the door minutes after the sheriff had departed. They listened to his car start and pull away.

Finally, Lucky asked, "Who's Jerry?"

"Sheriff's deputy," Annie answered. "We dated. Twice."

"Was it serious?"

She turned to glance at him, wary as could be. "I said we dated *twice*. How could that possibly be serious?" Her cheeks turned red. "Oh, you mean did we sleep together. No, absolutely not. If that's the question, we were not at all serious." She had the grace to look a little guilty. "And yes, I realize that word will be around town in a matter of hours, and everyone will think that I picked up a man in my store and brought him home. Believe it or not, that's preferable to having my friends and neighbors suspect the truth. Pancakes?" She headed for the kitchen, in her own unique way declaring the conversation over.

Lucky followed Annie to the kitchen. He really should just do what he'd been sent here to do and tell her that he couldn't help her. But in the back of his mind was a nagging, inescapable whisper he had never expected to encounter. *What if she's right?*

He stopped in the kitchen doorway and watched Annie

gather the ingredients for pancakes. She tried to hide the gentle tremble of her hands and the fear that lurked in her eyes as she set about making breakfast, but he saw.

She thought what she'd dreamed was real, and what if it was? What if, in spite of his grounded beliefs and perfectly logical *dis*belief, there was some way Annie's brain could pick up on thought waves, as if she were a human radio? She'd told him it was as if she were in the killer's head. She knew his mind, what he saw and thought.

Her brain was like a receiver. She'd said this had happened twice in her lifetime, and in both instances murder was involved. Violent murder and physical proximity. Bad things went on all the time, and yet Annie's receiver only activated when the violence happened within a certain distance. How close did she have to be?

He couldn't believe he was actually beginning to buy into her story, but in truth it was his only choice. Actually, he had two choices. He could believe her for the duration, or he could quit.

He watched Annie crack an egg into the pancake batter. She wore goofy, completely unsexy pajamas, and her hair was sticking out at all angles. Now and then, her toes with the pink-painted nails would curl a bit or tap against the tile floor, in sheer nervousness. She didn't ever wear makeup—at least, no more than a little lip gloss and mascara—and she didn't need it. Right now her bare face was as pretty as it had been when he'd first come to her door.

She kissed with an unexpected combination of innocence and passion. He liked her. He wanted her. He couldn't possibly quit.

Which meant he was going to have to believe.

"We're going to start all over," he said, crossing his arms over his bare chest as Annie turned her head to look at him.

"What do you mean?" she asked, never ceasing in her brisk whisking of the pancake batter.

"The answers we need won't come from the sheriff or the Huffs' relatives or anyone else but you. This begins and end with you, Annie."

"I still don't understand." The trepidation in her voice hinted that maybe she did understand…more than she wanted to.

"You're the key. In order to understand, we're going all the way back to the murder in Nashville."

Annie hadn't thought this could get any worse, but suddenly it was worse. She'd done her very best, for the past five years, to dismiss everything that had happened to her in Nashville, and now Lucky was making her relive it. All of it, from beginning to end.

Lucky had driven back to the bed-and-breakfast hours ago, showered and dressed, and returned with his pristine image and icy aura intact. She had never known a man who was so cool and collected and hard, but then, she'd never had reason to know a man of his type.

And once this was over, he'd be gone and she'd never know a man of his type again—she hoped. Not that she didn't like Lucky. She did. Too much. But trouble of a big kind had brought him here, and she didn't want trouble in her life.

She wanted peace. Quiet days. Good music. Laughing friends. Dreamless sleep. Was that too much to ask for?

When she'd finished telling him about the murder in Nashville, he reached a frightening conclusion that he shared with her in an emotionless voice. She didn't want to be a human radio tuned to violence, and she had no qualms about telling him so.

But looking back, after she calmed down a bit, she could see that he had some good points. The killer in Nashville had lived less than five miles from her apartment. She and the man who'd murdered his girlfriend could've been physically close at any time. At the grocery store, driving along the street, jogging, at the movie theater...anywhere.

If Lucky's theory was right, then at some point or another she'd been very close to the man who'd murdered the Huffs and had recently chosen a new set of victims. Did she know him? Had they said hello, bumped shoulders at the farmers' market, attended the summer festival at the same time, maybe eaten at the same restaurant? That idea gave her a deep chill that raised goose bumps on her arms. Did she know the killer? Is that why he'd invaded her dreams?

It was such a nice afternoon, they'd moved onto the back deck to work. Lucky looked out over the mountains, admiring the view she never got tired of or took for granted. He was quiet for a long time, stoic and still and about to explode, in his own quiet way. She suspected they did not want any of the same things from life. She wanted peace; peace would likely bore Lucky Santana silly. She was drawn to things that were different. Her clothing, her favorite music and her home all reflected that love of the unusual. Lucky was the most conservative man she'd ever met.

And yet they did have something in common. They were both lonely.

"I have an idea," he said, his gaze remaining fixed on the mountain view that seemed to stretch forever.

"What kind of idea?" She was almost afraid to know, and thankfully she was not reading his mind at the moment. For now, for this wonderful moment, her mind and her thoughts were her own. All was blessedly quiet in that respect.

Lucky turned his head and looked at her. Oh, there was so much power in those amber eyes, her heart lurched and her pulse sped up. Her mouth went dry. She remembered how he kissed, what he looked like without that conservative shirt, what he might look like wearing nothing at all. With a body and a face like that one, he likely had this effect on women of all ages and all types—compatibility be damned.

"You said this guy was drawn to the Huffs because they were happy, and that he's chosen a new couple to watch for the same reason. He wants what they have."

"Yes."

"And when he can't get it, he kills them."

She nodded, unable to speak.

Lucky gave her a heartbreaker smile. "Put on your dancing shoes, Annie Lockhart. We're about to become the happiest damn couple in Tennessee."

Chapter 6

Annie followed Lucky into the cabin, stepping through the kitchen door off the wide deck. He didn't have to be psychic to know she was close to panic.

"I understand your reasoning, but it'll never work," she said, her voice shallow and quick. "He's already picked his next victims. What makes you think he'll change his mind?"

"Got any better ideas?"

"Well, no, but…"

"What do we have to lose? We'll keep working to find his next victims and uncover his identity if you continue to have the dreams, and I'll continue to investigate the Huffs' deaths. If he comes to us, then it's just gravy."

"Gravy," Annie said beneath her breath. "A psycho might come after me, and you say it's gravy."

Lucky had almost reached the door that would lead him into the small dining area of the great room when he turned to look at her. Her vulnerability was at a new height, and he couldn't deny that it called to him in a primal way. If he didn't realize that the situation and the vulnerability were his weaknesses, he might think he was actually beginning to care about Annie Lockhart in a personal way. Right now, he really wanted to scoop her up and cover her body with his and go to the logical place that possessive move would take them.

But he did realize all his weaknesses, and that gave him the opportunity to push what he wanted deep. "I'm not going to let him get anywhere near you," he said.

"As if you're going to be here all the time," she countered, ending the statement with a very unladylike snort.

Obviously, she didn't yet get it. "I *will* be here all the time," he said. "If we're going to be that happy, I'm going to have to move in."

Her cheeks went pinker than usual, and her blue eyes danced—not with excitement, but with fear. "You're kidding, right?"

"I never kid. It's not in my hardwiring."

Her mouth opened and closed, as if she was trying to talk but couldn't. Finally she said, "If nothing else, no one will ever buy you and me as a couple, much less a happy one. We don't have anything in common."

"Haven't you ever heard that opposites attract?"

"I've *heard* it," she said. "I've just never *believed* it." She placed hands on hips and cocked one hip out, frustrated and scared—though she obviously didn't want him to know how she felt. She tried to appear tough, with that stance and the narrowed eyes and the firm lips. "Every successful couple I know are like two peas in a pod. They like the same movies and music, they dress in a similar fashion, they laugh at the same jokes. You and I have nothing in common," she said again, waving a dismissive hand in his direction. "No one who sees us together will ever buy—"

Lucky moved in smoothly and swiftly, catching Annie and pulling her to him, bending down to kiss her before she could take a breath and tell him to stop. Once her surprise faded, she melted in his arms. It was a gradual and decisive and complete surrender, until she was kissing him back with everything she had to give.

The kiss was soft and sweet, for a long moment, and then it turned into something deeper. Something more than a simple kiss. He felt Annie to his bones, and he wanted her. Here and now, he wanted her, personal weaknesses be damned.

One gentle hand crept to his neck and settled there, soft fingers oddly at home and familiar. Annie's body undulated slightly, moving closer to his own and remaining there, pressed against him in a move more sexual than the melding of their mouths. She was in his blood, just like that.

Nothing in common? Not true. He was in her blood, too.

Annie moved away slightly, breaking the kiss and laying her forehead against his shoulder. Her breath came hard and deep, and she held him as if she didn't want to let go.

Lucky cupped her neck in one hand and gently

forced her head back so she was looking him in the eye.
"They'll buy it," he whispered.

After a long, strained moment she answered with a
very reluctant "Okay."

Lucky insisted that for their ploy to work, it would
have to be very public. They couldn't expect the man
who was presently stalking another couple who was
blithely ignorant of his existence to drop by the cabin
and be suitably impressed. No, she and Lucky had to
get out and make sure everyone in Mercerville knew
they were now together.

He'd checked out of his room in Kristie's bed-and-
breakfast and moved his stuff into her spare bedroom.
Since her mother often stayed there, and was liable to
show up at any moment, it was relatively clean. She'd
just had to move a few of her supplies to the loft.

When that was done, he'd taken her to town. They
had reservations at Smokey's, but first they walked up
and down Main Street, holding hands and acting as if
they really were a couple. They window-shopped.
Lucky bought her fudge. Now and then he whispered
at her and ordered her to smile. As they were headed
for the restaurant he stopped on a street corner to kiss
her. In public. Quite thoroughly. He grabbed her ass
while he was kissing her.

She didn't need to call on any special powers to know
that people were watching. It occurred to her, too late, that
maybe the truth would've been better than this charade.

For the excursion to town she'd donned her favorite
skirt—a long, loose silk skirt in a variety of brightly

colored tie prints. It was topped with a turquoise tank top that sported a few sparklies around the neckline and a matching sweater. Instead of a pretty pair of sandals, which most women would've worn to complete the ensemble, she'd chosen to wear a clunky pair of soft brown boots. Fall was here, after all, so it was time to get her many pairs of boots out of the closet. She carried one of her own handbags, of course.

Lucky wore a black suit—no surprise—a white dress shirt, and what had to be the dullest tie ever made. And still, he was gorgeous. The artistic side of her brain mentally re-dressed him. Black jeans, very well worn. Motorcycle boots. A snug T-shirt. His hair a bit longer, and nicely mussed. She tried to make the image work, but it didn't make any more sense than her opting for a navy blue power suit and a pair of sensible pumps.

Besides, if he wore the outfit she envisioned for him, he wouldn't be able to hide the shoulder holster and gun he wore. She didn't like the fact that he was armed, but he'd informed her that until the man they were searching for was caught, he'd have his weapon close at all times.

They didn't look like any normal couple, but they did draw stares. That's what Lucky wanted, right? Attention. They were definitely drawing attention.

As far as she could tell, the man they were looking for hadn't seen them yet. She wished she had enough confidence in her ability to take some small comfort from that fact, but she didn't. What she saw or didn't see was so sporadic, it was little better than nothing at all. Only the dreams were strong enough to be called reliable. The random thoughts that came to her head were erratic.

Tonight, they were blessedly absent.

Smokey's was the best restaurant in town. Since there were so many tourists in the area year-round, it was also casual. In his suit, Lucky stood out like a sore thumb. Everyone stared. People she knew; complete strangers; women of all ages. She had a feeling he would draw stares no matter where he went or what he wore. He was just the kind of man who stood out in a crowd.

A part of her was still convinced that no one would ever buy them as a couple. Lucky Santana was fantasy material. She was not. But like it or not, the chemistry was there. On her side of the equation, anyway.

When Lucky reached across their small table and covered her hand with his, a decided chill crawled up her arm and settled in her throat. Yeah, that was definitely chemistry.

"You're not smiling," he whispered in a low voice no one else could hear.

"That's because I'm terrified your ploy will work," she answered, her voice no louder than his.

He turned her hand over and began to rock his thumb against her palm. *Oh, my.* "I might have brought in a female Benning agent to play your part, but since you lied to the sheriff about us this morning—" he shrugged slightly "—you are the logical choice. Don't worry. No one's going to get close to you. I called Murphy this afternoon, and he's sending some of his new toys. They'll be here tomorrow."

"Toys?" She could feel herself blush. "For goodness' sake, Lucky. What makes you think we have any need for…*toys?*"

Lucky's grin widened. It was positively wicked. It was the kind of smile women sighed and responded to, the kind of smile that felt as if it became a tangible thing and leapt into a woman's gut. She felt it there, in her stomach and in the chills on her arms.

"Not the kind of toys you're thinking about, Annie, dear. Though if you're so inclined..." Again that subtle shrug.

"You're enjoying this," she accused.

His amber eyes went hard. "Damn straight."

They had a very nice dinner. Lucky ate well. Annie found that nothing on her plate had any taste, and what little she did eat she had to choke down. How had everything in her life gotten so out of hand? And it was terribly and completely out of hand. There was a killer loose in Mercerville, and no one but Lucky would ever believe her. This killer who had invaded her dreams had chosen his next victims, and Lucky was determined that they should step into the psycho's line of vision and take their place.

Worse, she was developing entirely inappropriate feelings for an entirely inappropriate man.

While she toyed with her crème brûlée, Lucky sipped coffee. Now and then he glanced around the table and down. Finally, he settled his gaze on her boots and sighed. "Is that what you call dancing shoes?"

"I don't dance," she said, lifting a small bite of dessert to her mouth. "At least, not in public. When I dance it's alone, in the safety of my own house where no one else can see."

"That bad, huh?"

"Yes." She offered him a bite of her dessert. "Don't you want a taste?"

He shook his head.

She didn't lower the spoon. "Come on. It'll look very sexy to anyone who's watching."

"When you change the subject, you do so very abruptly," he said. "Have you never heard of the segue?"

"I feel like an idiot, sitting here with my hand out and you practically ignoring me," she responded, waggling the spoon so that the crème brûlée danced. "It certainly doesn't paint a pretty picture. I hope the man we're looking for isn't watching."

Lucky leaned forward slowly, tilting toward her. He opened his mouth, and it approached the spoon she held. Very slowly, he closed his lips over the spoon and pulled back, taking the dessert into his mouth. The ingestion of one bite of food should not be sexy, but something deep inside her tilted and whirled. Her heart thumped too hard.

"Satisfied?" Lucky asked when his mouth was once again empty.

Not even a little. "Yes, thank you." She shoveled another bite into her mouth, not nearly so gracefully as Lucky.

All day her recently awakened ability had remained blessedly silent, but now, looking at Lucky across the table, she was once again assaulted by the image of his body above hers, the fan whirring, the scar on his shoulder. As visions went it was very nice…even though she knew this man could break her heart without breaking a sweat.

She was going to have to remind herself frequently

that no matter how far they went with this charade, he didn't love her and never would. It was work, a game, perhaps even a diversion.

If she was smart she wouldn't let this make-believe romance go that far, but she had a feeling her intelligence or lack thereof had nothing to do with her relationship with Lucky Santana.

Upon returning to the cabin, Annie had changed into a pair of faded jeans and a T-shirt that said If You Can Read This, You're Standing Too Close. Her way of telling him to keep a distance when they were in private, or complete coincidence? He couldn't be sure. This plan definitely had her antsy.

Lucky had removed his jacket and tie and put aside the shoulder holster and pistol, but that was his only concession to comfort, as he made a few phone calls on his cell and studied the Huff case file.

Annie passed the evening curled up in her favorite chair with a large sketch pad sitting on her lap. A fire burned low in the stone fireplace, a welcome and cozy addition on a cool night. Annie said she was working, but from Lucky's vantage point it looked as if she was passing the time doodling so she wouldn't have to deal with him.

"I'd like to place an order," he said after a long bout of silence.

Annie's head popped up. "What kind of an order?"

"You make bags, right?"

"I design and manufacture handbags."

"That's what I said."

She looked thoroughly disgusted. "So, what is this? A gift for your girlfriend?"

"I don't have a girlfriend. You know that."

"Mother?"

He felt his jaw tighten. "Dead. Look, all I want is a pretty diaper bag for…"

"Diaper bag?" She dropped the sketch pad. "I don't design diaper bags!"

She sounded absolutely insulted. "Why not? I want something about so big." He gestured with his hands. "I guess it should be pink, maybe with some froufrou girlie stuff like the bag you carried tonight, and it should have dividers on the inside so the baby crap can be organized. I want an outer pocket with a Velcro fastener." He reached for the holster he'd deposited on the table beside his chair and smoothly drew the pistol out, holding it up so Annie could see. "The pocket should be about this size, and there should be a built-in holster that—"

"Hold it." Annie lifted her hand in a motion meant to demand silence. "You want me to design a diaper bag with a special compartment for a *gun*?"

"Yeah."

"That's ridiculous."

"I don't think so."

"You're warped."

"I'm sure Sadie wouldn't go to the Piggly Wiggly armed, but you never know when you might need access to a diaper and a weapon."

In disgust, she snatched up her sketch pad and dismissed his request. "You need serious psychological help," she said without looking at him.

"Something we have in common."

Annie returned to her doodling, and Lucky leaned back in his chair and watched. They had more in common than either of them would admit. Best not to go there, he supposed.

He was staring into the fire moments later when Annie spoke in a more level tone of voice. "Sadie. She's the one, right?"

"The one what?" he snapped.

"The one you sometimes think you're in love with. That song 'Sexy Sadie' popped into my head, and when I hummed it you looked like I'd slapped you. You even asked once who told me about Sadie. Sometimes you think you missed the boat with her, that if you'd made your move before she met—"

"I didn't give you permission to go poking around in my brain," he snapped.

"I'm not," Annie said. "At least, not right now. Everything's quiet at the moment, which is very nice. And now you're the one changing the subject. Tell me about Sadie." The question was offered casually, but he suspected there was nothing casual about it. "I'm guessing she has a baby, a girl, since you requested a pink diaper bag."

"She has a baby girl and a little boy. We were partners for years. I never thought I'd trust a woman to watch my back, but Sadie was sharp. She was a good shot, quick on her feet, smart." He grinned. "Sassy, too."

"So, you two were…" Annie lifted one hand and waggled her fingers. The pencil she was holding danced.

"Never," Lucky said emphatically. "I wouldn't ruin a good, solid work relationship with sex. Sex is easy to find. Someone you can truly trust, that's another story." He snorted. "And then she has to go and fall in love and get married and make babies. It's disgusting."

Annie smiled widely. "You never loved Sadie. You like her, and you don't really *like* many women, so you were easily and understandably confused."

"I like women just fine," Lucky argued in a steady voice.

"You like women as a gender. You admire them, but you don't want any one to get too close. Liking women and liking a woman isn't the same thing, and you know it. You like Sadie and you trust her, and I understand that trust doesn't come easily to you. Sadie's in a good place. She's found what she spent half her life searching for. If you really care about your old partner, you'll be happy for her."

"I am," he said defensively. And then he added, in a softer voice, "Most of the time."

"So—" Annie started doodling again "—I can see that you don't want to talk about Sadie. What about your mother? You said she was dead. When did she pass?"

Old, nasty feelings rose up and threatened to choke him. "Not tonight."

"Okay." She didn't sound surprised at his refusal.

Was she peeking inside him right now, searching for his deepest secrets? Lucky didn't think so. She was too relaxed at the moment. In the past, when she'd claimed to be having some sort of vision, she'd been strained and pale. Right now she was peaceful and pretty, with her feet bare dangling and that sketch pad in her lap, and the fire giving her face a glow that was warm and soft and almost eerie.

"A couple of guys from the agency will be here tomorrow afternoon," he said in a businesslike tone of voice. "The surveillance equipment will be set up and operational by tomorrow night."

"Your toys," she said with a half smile.

"My toys."

Lucky reached for the pitifully thin and inadequate folder the sheriff had delivered that morning, and opened it to peruse information he'd already digested. Twice.

So, who was changing the subject now?

Behind a closed bedroom door, Annie threw on her Drama Queen T-shirt and opened the curtains at the wide window that looked over the mountains. Would Lucky sleep tonight? Would she?

She didn't worry about anyone watching her through the window. Not only was her bedroom dark, there was nothing beyond her window but the mountains she'd come to love. It was so unfair that something as ugly as murder could touch this beautiful place.

A part of her wished she didn't know. Ignorance was bliss, truly. But since she did know, she had to do something. If that meant parading around town on Lucky Santana's arm, pretending to be in love, then that's what she'd do. She just hoped she wouldn't forget that it was all pretend.

She delayed going to sleep, because she was afraid of the dreams that might come. Murder or Lucky?

Violence and death or sexual fantasies? She knew which dream she'd prefer, but she wouldn't have any choice in the matter. Whatever would come would come. Since she had no choice but to sleep, all she could do was hope that tonight's dreams would be good ones.

In a way, she found comfort in Lucky's theory about her abilities, even though it basically made her a human radio receiver that was tuned to the murderer channel. If there was a physical reason for her visions, she wouldn't feel so much like a freak. If he was right, then she'd inherited a physical trait from her grandmother, not a freakish, inexplicable aberration. Not that anyone else would buy Lucky's explanation.

But she'd know.

Today had been a good day. Her mind had remained quiet. Maybe last night's nightmare vision had drained her abilities, for a while. She didn't expect that would last. The dreams wouldn't stop until they caught the killer, but the respite was nice.

She crawled into the bed, and for a while she listened to Lucky move about the cabin. He probably wouldn't go to sleep for hours. What had he been thinking to drink all that coffee so near to bedtime? He probably had all sorts of bad habits she didn't know about. Not yet, anyway. They were living together, so eventually she'd get to see all of them.

Annie gazed up at the fan above her bed, and for a moment—just one crazy moment—she wished for the rest of her vision to come true. She wanted Lucky hovering above her, holding her…inside her. She wanted everything. Sex for the sake of sex, a closeness that was much more than physical, a friend to reach for when the bad dreams came. What would Lucky say if she left the bed right now and asked him to sleep with her?

He'd say yes, of course, and then she'd be lost. She wanted much more than he had to give.

She closed her eyes, and headed toward sleep with the comforting thought that maybe the man who'd killed the Huffs had changed his mind about the happy couple he'd been watching and admiring lately, and had already moved on. Not to her and Lucky, but to another town. Another state.

The thought was not so comforting when she reminded herself that if that happened before she and Lucky identified him, the psycho would kill again. She knew without doubt that he'd kill again, and he'd keep killing until he was caught. If she'd been given this ability for a reason, then she couldn't wish the murderer away.

Her life had been so blessedly simple before the dreams and Lucky Santana had made their appearances. Now, it was anything but.

Chapter 7

Early in the afternoon, Murphy and one of the new guys showed up to install the surveillance equipment—and to ask too damned many questions. Lucky didn't tell them any more than he had to. He found himself in a tricky situation. A part of him believed in Annie and her abilities, but he had no proof. He had nothing concrete to take to the agency in order to request more men and more equipment. He had nothing that made any logical sense.

Lucky Santana was all about logic, or at least he had been until coming here.

With his work almost done, Murphy made the observation that the client was cute. The new guy agreed with an apelike grunt. Lucky chose not to respond to either.

When the surveillance equipment—cameras and alarms at the perimeter of Annie's property—was set up, Lucky sent Murphy and the new guy on their way and started making phone calls. He knew a lot of law-enforcement people in the Southeast, some of them well enough to approach unofficially. According to the file on the Huff case, the findings at the scene hadn't given the investigators any reason to believe what had happened was anything other than a murder/suicide. True, the country investigators weren't exactly a team of experts, but still…the killer hadn't made any notice-able mistakes.

Which meant that maybe he'd done this before.

Lucky called a few old friends and acquaintances, and asked if they'd had any murder/suicides in the past couple of years that were in any way fishy. He hadn't heard back from anyone yet. If they came to him with a case or cases that were similar, then what?

Then things would really get ugly, that's what. People higher up would have to be called if he had any evidence that there was a serial killer out there working undetected. If that happened, they'd want to know what had turned him on to these cases. Like it or not, it all came back to Annie. Even if he didn't tell everything—and he wouldn't have any choice in that matter—Cal knew how this investigation had started.

He was worrying about something that might not happen. For now, all he had was a pretty girl, a few bad dreams and a suspicious case that had not been handled well by the locals.

Annie hadn't had any disturbing dreams in a couple

of days. She seemed relieved not to be assaulted by the nightmares, but her serene nights didn't help the case at all. No one had returned Lucky's phone calls, the case file told him nothing and there was apparently no crime at all in Mercerville—much less murder.

The weekend meant high visibility. If he was right and the murderer had at one point been in Annie's immediate vicinity, and the psycho was currently tracking someone in Mercerville, then odds were he would see the new happy couple and be intrigued. Would it be enough to draw him in?

This was a risk, a dangerous game, but Lucky didn't doubt he could handle the man who'd murdered the Huffs. Trey Huff had not been prepared for violence; Lucky was always prepared.

Friday night he and Annie had gone to dinner again, eating at a more casual restaurant this time. Saturday they'd spent the day downtown—part of the time in Annie's shop, the rest of the time being as publicly affectionate as possible. At one point, while Annie had been deep in conversation with her manager, Lucky had made a quick run to the pharmacy two doors down. There he'd purchased a soft drink—and a few condoms. He didn't think he'd have any use for the condoms, but the purchase was good for the image they were trying to present.

On Sunday he took Annie to the park at the edge of town, where a large number of residents and tourists had gathered to watch the leaves change colors, picnic and toss various discs and balls around.

They claimed a bench where they could see and be

seen, and Lucky draped his arm familiarly over Annie's shoulder.

It was beginning to feel very natural, to hold her this way. He was even getting accustomed to her apparently vast collection of boots. Today she wore well-worn jeans, a T-shirt adorned with sequined flowers and soft brown, clunky boots. Since they were coming to the park and a suit wouldn't do, he'd settled for khakis, a golf shirt and an ankle holster. Before they'd left the cabin, Annie had accused him—again—of dressing like her father. As usual, she'd tossed the accusation at him with a wide smile.

"I never got the appeal of the whole autumn thing," he said as his gaze raked the park for signs of suspicious behavior. He saw none. "Leaves change colors. They do it every year about this time, so what's the big deal?"

Annie laughed lightly, "You're not exactly Nature Boy, are you?"

"Nope. Give me the great indoors any day."

She relaxed, resting her head on his shoulder very casually and easily, and he had to remind himself that this was all make-believe. They weren't romantically involved, she wasn't his type, they weren't "happy." It was just for show that he raked his fingers through her hair.

"Have you ever stood at the edge of a lake or an ocean, watched the sunlight sparkle there and been amazed?" she asked gently. "Have you ever stood beneath a night sky and marveled at the stars? To me, and to others I suppose, the changing leaves are like that. They're beautiful in a way so well beyond what we recognize as beautiful that they take my breath away."

Lucky wasn't big on admiring beauty, unless there was a female concerned. Now was probably not the time to make that observation.

She straightened considerably and he dropped his hand from her hair, as a familiar couple approached. Kristie Bentley's grin was insanely wide. Her husband, Stu, looked as if he were being dragged across the park. Lucky stood to greet the couple, and so did Annie. In order to make things look really good, Lucky took Annie's hand in his and held on tight. A less observant man might've missed the gentle tremor of her fingers.

"Hey, you two," the perky brunette called as she drew near, her grin growing even wider. The way her eyes flitted from Lucky to Annie, it was clear that she definitely bought the two of them as a couple. Since Kristie knew Annie well, she was likely not alone in that respect. The ploy was working. "What are y'all doing this afternoon?"

"Admiring the leaves," Lucky said, and then he shrugged his shoulders slightly, telling anyone who cared to pay attention that he was here only to please his lady love.

"It's such a nice day," Annie said. "We thought we'd, you know, get out of the cabin."

Where it was likely believed they'd been having wild monkey sex for days, now. What a shame that wasn't true.

"What are y'all doing Tuesday night?" Kristie asked. "You really should come down to the house and have supper with us. There's a group staying with us for the week, and they're making a trip to Gatlinburg on Tuesday. They won't be back until late, so we won't be at all busy."

Annie looked to Lucky, searching for a clue as to how she should answer.

"Honey," Stu said in a low, calm voice as he draped his arm over his wife's shoulder, "I'm sure they have other things to do besides—"

"Oh, they do not," Kristie interrupted, leaning into her husband in a familiar way. "Everyone has to eat. They might as well eat with us."

Annie was obviously hesitant to answer. Maybe she was afraid the charade they were pulling off in public would be much more difficult with a friend. Maybe she'd feel like she had to tell Kristie and Stu the truth, if they spent any significant amount of time together. He'd disabuse her of that notion later, just in case her mind had headed in that direction.

Again, Annie looked at him with that questioning expression on her face. To anyone watching, that glance would look very intimate, when in truth it was all business.

Well, almost all business.

"Dinner Tuesday would be great," Lucky said. "What time?"

The women took care of the details with a couple of short, familiar sentences, in that way close friends are able to do. Stu looked slightly uncomfortable and a little apologetic. No man wanted to interfere in another man's early-relationship wild-monkey sex.

When Kristie and Stu moved on, Lucky and Annie reclaimed their bench. They tried to salvage their earlier, comfortable position, but it couldn't be recreated. After a few minutes, Annie said, "I don't know what's going on, but the hairs on the back of my neck are standing up."

Lucky didn't say anything, but he felt the same odd chill.

Someone was watching.

A small part of Annie knew, when she crawled into bed on Sunday evening, that her dreams that night would not be of the pleasant sort. This afternoon in the park she'd felt the killer watching. If Lucky was right about physical proximity playing a role, how could she escape this night untouched by the nightmares of the killer's mind? She knew what was coming, and still she fell asleep quickly.

As usual, the dreams were disjointed and alarming and very real. She was in the killer's head…and she was watching herself.

His thoughts were so twisted, she had a hard time making sense of them. He felt entitled to something that wasn't his, and he lived with an anger that never went away. He hid his rage well, behind smiles and kind words, but the anger was always there, simmering. Growing. All-consuming.

Only one thing would make the rage subside, for a while.

Annie woke with a start and sat up in the bed, looking at the bedside clock and hoping the night was done. It wasn't even two-thirty yet, but she didn't want to go back to sleep. The dream wasn't finished. It would come again, beginning right where it had ended, if she went back to sleep.

Instead of lying down, she threw off the covers and stood, allowing the cool night air to brush her bare legs and arms and wake her up. This afternoon in the park, she'd known the killer had seen her. She and Lucky had walked around the park after that, but no other useful sensations had come to her, and they hadn't seen anyone suspicious. She saw people she knew—friends and acquaintances. Was the man who'd invaded her head one of them? The postman or the bag boy from the grocery store. The preacher or the economics teacher from the high school. A husband, a son, a father…*who*?

She opened the door and stepped into the hallway. The television wasn't on, so maybe Lucky had already gone to bed. He often stayed up very late, and she'd been hoping he was still awake so she could talk to him for a while. She'd tell him the dream—give it to him the way she'd given him her problems—and then maybe she could sleep without interruption.

The door to the spare bedroom was almost closed, but not quite. Lucky left it open at night so he could hear everything that was going on in the cabin. If anyone stepped onto her property, they'd know it. An alarm would sound. Cameras would click. No one was going to get close to the house, but that didn't mean he'd rest easy.

Did he ever?

She pushed the door farther open, and as she did Lucky rolled over and opened his eyes. His room was dim but she could see him well enough, thanks to the night-light in the hallway. He didn't look at all sleepy, and she wondered if he'd been lying there awake all this time.

"He saw us today," she whispered.

"I know." Lucky sat up, and Annie moved farther into the room.

"He didn't choose us, but we have grabbed his attention." She looked down, into those hard eyes that had captured her from the beginning. The light here was too low for her to see and admire the color, but she knew what they looked like by bright light and dim. "I know that's what we wanted, but…it's scary. I don't want him to watch us. I don't want him anywhere near either of us."

"You're shaking," he said.

"I'm cold." To reinforce that statement, Annie hugged her arms and ran hands up and down in a search for warmth.

A better method of warming herself was waiting. Lucky drew down the covers and scooted to the other side of the bed, making room for her. She shouldn't think of crawling into that bed. He shouldn't ask. But she didn't hesitate before slipping beneath the covers, into a bed that had been nicely warmed by Lucky's body heat.

He stayed on his side of the mattress. "Tell me about the dream."

"Do I have to?"

He hesitated a moment. "No. It can wait until morning, unless you dreamed a name and address."

She actually laughed a little, something she'd thought impossible just a moment ago. "No, sorry."

"Go on back to sleep, then. We'll talk about it in the morning."

"I don't really want to go back to sleep." She realized the possible meaning of those words the moment they were out of her mouth. She was, after all, in Lucky's bed, and there were other things they could do here besides sleep. She'd dreamed about those things. She'd even had visions. "I mean, I'm afraid I might dream about the killer again, and even though you need to know as much as possible, I don't want to dream about him again, ever."

"I know what you mean." There was a touch of humor in his voice. He knew very well she was embarrassed by her poor choice of words.

She rolled onto her side so her back was to Lucky, and she sighed deeply. "I wish I was normal."

"You're as normal as any woman I've ever known," he responded, his voice rumbling softly. "You just happen to know stuff other women don't."

"That's simplifying the matter substantially."

"Doesn't mean it's not true."

And then he was there, his breath on her neck and his hand on her waist. She held her breath, waiting for what would come next, but Lucky didn't make a move. He simply settled down there, too close for comfort, not close enough to suit her.

"If you have a bad dream tonight, when you wake up I'll be here. Right here, Annie. You've tapped into something bad and scary, I get that, but there's no one here but you and me. He can't hurt you."

No, but you can. She didn't say that aloud, and she didn't move away. She could move, if she wanted to, but she liked the feel of Lucky's body so close. She liked the solidness and the body heat and the dip of the mattress.

Most of all, she liked not facing these visions alone.

So instead of moving away, she allowed herself to

relax against Lucky's hard, warm body. Her back molded to his chest. He wasn't wearing a shirt or pajama top. His chest was beautifully bare, marred only by that scar on his shoulder. Beneath the covers, maybe he wore underwear for sleeping. Maybe there were plain flannel pajama bottoms. Then again, maybe he wore nothing at all. Her hand itched to reach down and back to see what she might find…but of course she didn't.

It was foolish to be here in this bed. It would be foolish beyond reason to take the opportunity to explore.

"Good night, Lucky," she said.

"Good night, Annie. Sweet dreams."

She sighed. "Very funny."

And then, within minutes, the sleep she'd been dreading came upon her swiftly.

How could she do that? How could Annie crawl into his bed and almost immediately go to sleep?

The attraction between them had been there from the beginning, and it increased every day. Of course it did. They were two healthy, unattached adults living in the same freakin' house. They held hands, they touched in public, they spent every waking hour together. And now here they were in an *un*waking hour.

Sex with Annie Lockhart was going to be a mistake, but that didn't mean he didn't think it was going to happen. Soon.

But not soon enough.

Lucky did doze, eventually, but he kept waking to see

if Annie had moved—away or closer. It was near dawn when he came awake to find her restless. She whispered. *No.* Her body, which had been so wonderfully relaxed, tensed and curled inward, and instinctively she moved away from him.

There was no doubt that he should let the dream run its course. She might learn something important this time. Not the name and address he'd asked her for, but some detail he could use to track down the culprit. He watched her for a few moments, and she grew increasingly more distressed. Her body was tense, the noises she made were pitiful and frightened.

It was the tear that pushed him over the edge. By the soft light of a night-light that burned beyond his opened bedroom door, he saw a single teardrop slip from the corner of her eye.

Rising up on his elbow, Lucky took her arm and shook it gently. "Annie, wake up," he whispered.

She didn't immediately do as he instructed. In fact, she seemed to grow more distressed, as if he had only intensified the effects of the nightmare.

He called her name again, in a slightly louder voice. She'd pushed the covers down to just below her waist. The T-shirt she wore to sleep in had ridden up to her belly button, bunching there just beneath the words Drama Queen and offering him just a glimpse of skin. It was skin he'd seen before, since she was fond of small shirts and low-riding jeans, but somehow this was different. Of course it was different. She was in his bed, and when a woman came to a man's bed everything changed.

His hand slipped just beneath the shirt and settled on her taut stomach. She was warm, and he could feel the pounding of her heart in her soft skin. "Wake up."

She did, with a gasp and the flinging of one arm, an arm he caught and held steady as she came awake.

Her eyes caught and held his, and in an instant he saw her fear, her surprise and finally her relief. She relaxed very quickly, then she closed her eyes and took a deep, cleansing breath. "He's closer," she whispered.

"To the couple he's been watching, or to us?" Lucky asked. He didn't release her arm, but dropped it down slowly.

"I don't know."

In order for this moment to end as it should one of them needed to move away, but neither did. At the moment, Annie was grateful not to be alone, and Lucky was unable to move. Not only was he inescapably drawn to Annie, he needed to stay under the covers until his extremely inconvenient erection went away.

Some women were pretty in the morning; others weren't. Annie was actually more beautiful, with her hair mussed and her face warmly flushed with sleep. Her eyes were clear, her cheeks nicely pink. Maybe she was a morning person. Maybe she was just so naturally pretty that she never had to worry about puffy eyes or annoying lines. Some women painted on their beauty. Annie's beauty was natural. It came from a place deep inside her, and straight from sleep it shone from her.

As they lay there, face-to-face, closer than they had ever been before, Annie's expression changed. Her eyes narrowed and her lips parted slightly. He knew that look. Her head cocked to one side as she studied him, and she reached out to touch his face with soft fingers that trailed along his stubbled jaw.

"I usually try to wash my dreams away with a shower."

"That sounds like a good idea." Maybe if she'd get out of his bed and get her hand off his face, he'd quit thinking about ripping that silly T-shirt off her body and tasting every inch of her.

"But this is better." That hand trailed down to his neck, and then to his chest. "It's nice, to be held. To wake up from a nightmare to…to this."

In that maddening way she had, she immediately changed the subject. "Where did you get the scar?" Her fingers traced the thin, old line on his shoulder.

"Bar fight," he answered simply.

Annie smiled, just a little. It was a soft, natural, sexy smile. "Never lie to a psychic, Lucky, even a bad one. You never know when you'll get caught." She closed her eyes and took one long, deep breath, while one finger continued to trace the scar. Back and forth. Back and forth. "You were very young, and very angry, and the knife hurt more than you thought it would." Her smile faded and she caught her breath, as if she'd been surprised. "I'm sorry."

He took her wrist in his hand and drew it away from the scar, before she saw too much.

"Annie…"

"I know. We should stop before it's too late. We should ignore the fact that this little charade feels more real every day. We should shake hands and be business-like and take lots of cold showers."

"Lots of 'shoulds' there."

His hand instinctively returned to her partially exposed midsection, and settled there. Her hand returned to his chest, but she didn't touch the scar again.

She should leave the bed, but he didn't want her to go.

"We both know it's going it happen before you leave," she whispered. "We're going to…" She hesitated, searching for the right words. *Have sex. Make love. Get off. Do it. Give in.* "I would say sleep together," she finished, "but we've already done that and that's not what I mean, in the literal sense. It's going to happen, now, or tonight, or tomorrow or next weekend. So, why wait? I know you're not going to stay, so you don't have to worry about unrealistic expectations or that nasty commitment you don't want. I'm not stupid. I probably understand you better than any woman you've ever known. I'm not trying to trap you or make this relationship more than it is. I don't expect you to…I don't expect anything." She moved a little closer. "But I need you in more ways than you can imagine, and I know you want me."

"You do?"

In an unusually bold move, Annie reached beneath the covers and stroked his erection with the tips of her fingers. "I do."

He was much too far gone to argue with her. "Busted."

Chapter 8

Lucky's hand very slowly crept beneath her shirt, climbing up her torso a fraction of an inch at a time. Annie felt herself melting into the mattress, melting against the hard body of the man who held her. Just…melting.

His fingers found and teased her breasts, flicking over the sensitive nipples. Her physical reaction to that caress was surprisingly intense, and Annie heard herself gasp. Her eyes drifted closed, and she drank in the sensations of being touched, of being loved.

She'd never been intimate with a man while her psychic abilities were active, so for a moment or two she wondered if this closeness would lead to jarring and too-personal images and thoughts that would fill her mind until she could see nothing else. But her thoughts remained her own, as Lucky continued to touch her, as he lowered his head to kiss the side of her neck and set a riot of new sensations into motion.

Her body throbbed, and she wanted him now. But oh, she didn't want this time to pass too quickly. She wanted to savor every second…every sensation.

Annie didn't just want to be touched, she wanted to be the one doing the touching, too. And she did. Her hands explored and caressed and aroused, just as Lucky's did. She touched his skin and kissed his shoulder and the side of his powerful neck, finding and tasting his pulse there. She traced nicely honed muscles with her fingertips—Lucky had a chest that sported some crisp black chest hairs, but not too many—and then she tasted those same places, trailing the tip of her tongue here and there. She learned his body, she made him moan, the way he made her moan. And then her hand delved once again beneath the covers.

Boxers. Why was she not surprised?

Lucky lifted her into a half-sitting position and removed her T-shirt. Her sleepwear was tossed aside and she was left mostly naked and caught under his intent perusal.

"Perfect," he said as his fingers traced her breasts.

Annie knew she was anything but perfect, but for the moment she remained silent. For now, for this moment in time, she could pretend that they were both perfect in every way. She was beautiful and without any abnormal abilities. Lucky wasn't afraid of being caught in a woman's web; he knew the difference between trust and love—and he could offer her both. She wanted both, and she wanted them from him. It was a grating thought, and she was very glad that he couldn't peek into her brain, the way she could sometimes peek into his.

He couldn't ever know that in the predawn hours, while he aroused her with his hands and his mouth, love entered her mind and her heart. She hadn't lied to him; she wouldn't ask for more than he had to give. That didn't mean the possibility of more couldn't tease her.

The room grew warm; the covers and what was left of their clothing—her panties and his boxers—were shed and tossed aside. That wasn't the end of the touching; it was just the beginning, as if they started the process all over again. There was something about lying against a man, totally naked and close—so close—to taking him into her body. It went beyond intimacy...beyond sexual fulfillment. This was trust—complete and primal.

When Annie thought she couldn't possibly be more aroused, Lucky found a new place to caress or kiss her. He was without inhibition, and for the moment so was she. In many ways, it didn't feel like a first time. There was no awkwardness—no reticence on her part or his.

And then, it was time. She knew it instinctively, and so did Lucky. He very quickly, without a single wasted movement, retrieved a condom from his small suitcase. While he was out of the bed, for those few seconds, Annie admired his bare body. It was perfectly formed, hard and nicely shaped and manly, with long muscular legs and slim hips and a *very* nice ass. He was impressively aroused. The only scar she saw was the one on his shoulder. He truly was perfect.

"You travel prepared," she said as he rejoined her in the bed.

"I bought a box at the pharmacy in Mercerville," he said, as his heaviness settled over her body in a beautiful and natural way.

"You did?"

"I bought lots." His head lowered and he kissed her neck again. She responded by wrapping her legs around his and gently pulling him closer. "I thought it would be good for our image," he murmured against her throat.

Instead of giving her what she wanted and entering her *now,* Lucky pulled away slightly and took one hard nipple into his mouth. He suckled and nipped and teased, and she settled her hands in his hair and held on tight. Her body began to rock slightly, as if he were already inside her. Her hips rose and fell, and a gentle tremor traveled from her head to her toes.

If he kept going, she was going to orgasm before the lovemaking actually began.

No, this had been *lovemaking* from the moment he'd slipped his hand beneath her nightshirt.

Lucky's hand glided between their bodies and touched her. He stroked as he had earlier, bringing her to the brink and then gentling his touch. Could he feel her tremble? Did he know she was literally shaking with need?

With Lucky's mouth on her breast and his fingers working magic between her legs, Annie came. Hard. Her body bucked, she made a noise she did not recognize as her own. She held on to Lucky with all her might as the sensations whipped through her body.

Outside the bedroom window, dawn was upon them. When she opened her eyes she could see Lucky's face well. He was watching her so intently, she felt certain there was more intimacy in that gaze than there was in the sexual exploration of his mouth and hands.

While his eyes and hers were locked, he entered her. She was wet, trembling, receptive. One long stroke, and she once again felt the need growing inside her. She closed her eyes and lost herself in the rhythm of making love. It was a lovely rhythm, and she soon forgot everything else but the way Lucky made her feel.

Every inch of her skin was sensitive, exposed and quivering. Her hips and his met, again and again, and there was no thought involved. It was so right; so natural. There was a primitiveness to the way they made love, as if every move, every breath, was instinctive and inescapable and wholly *theirs*.

Again, she felt the beginning wave of orgasm. Lucky drove deeper than before; he touched her in a place that grasped and fluttered in response to his thrust, and she came with a sharp cry. Lucky came with her, this time.

All night, Annie's thoughts had been hers and hers alone, but it seemed that she shared Lucky's climax with him. Not in her head, but throughout her entire body. The experience took her to a new and unexpected place, and for a while—a few seconds or a few minutes, she couldn't be sure—she was transported to a place where nothing existed but the two of them.

For that short and wonderful time, she was filled with the knowledge that this man was hers, and always would be.

But a few minutes later, when he left the bed, she had to remind herself that Lucky would only be hers for a short time. A very short time.

It was an unfortunate fact of life that women some-times—often, to be honest—made too much out of a little fun sex. Lucky would like to think otherwise, but he had a feeling Annie was one of those women. Yeah, he had been attracted to her from the start, and she'd been attracted to him, so maybe what had happened last night had been inevitable. That didn't mean anything had to change. He worked for her; she wasn't his type.

In truth, sex always changed everything with women. Why couldn't they be like men and just appreciate sex for the physical pleasure?

He'd explored every inch of her body, and found no tattoos. Not a single one. In a way he was surprised. No tattoo meant his initial read of her had been wrong. He was never wrong, not where women were concerned. Not anymore.

Lucky made his own breakfast. Cereal. Annie slept late. He worried incessantly about what she'd say when she finally got out of bed. If there were hugs and kisses and declarations of love—shudder—he'd have to make some serious changes around here.

Maybe he could reason with her. Ha.

It was after ten when she finally woke. He heard the shower running, and geared himself up to do battle, if necessary. Earlier this morning she'd caught him half-asleep and hard, and that explained away everything. The sex had been good, and she'd come like a woman who'd never had an orgasm before. He hoped that wasn't the case. Women tended to get very clingy when they had their first climax.

Annie soon headed into the kitchen, where Lucky was washing his breakfast dishes. Her hair was in that always-mussed style he was getting accustomed to. She wore her favorite pair of jeans, which were very faded and had a small frayed hole in the right thigh. Today she wore a green T-shirt with long, loose sleeves that had lace around the cuff. Her slender feet were bare. Her toenails had been painted red a few days ago. He liked them well enough, though he did think the pink polish was prettier on her.

Like he cared what color her toenails were.

He steeled himself for some emotional confrontation, as Annie headed to the refrigerator. She came out with a container of yogurt, and then grabbed a spoon from the silverware drawer.

"I'm starving this morning," she said as she claimed a seat at the small kitchen table. "I guess that's what I get for sleeping so late."

"Yeah," Lucky said as he finished drying his cereal bowl.

"What's the plan for today?" she asked, and then she attacked her yogurt with relish.

"We'll go to your shop for a while and have lunch in town. This afternoon I need to make a few more phone calls."

"To see if you can find out if the man who murdered the Huffs has done this before," she said.

He had hesitated in mentioning that possibility to

her, but since it was possible anything she knew might trigger a vision, he'd told her of his suspicions days ago. Not that it had helped. So far she couldn't tell him if the man they were looking for had killed once or a hundred times.

He made an affirmative sound as he put the bowl away.

"We should go to the café across the street for lunch," Annie said brightly. "They have great salads, and all this eating out is beginning to tell. I think I gained two pounds last week."

"You can afford to gain two more," he said. As far as he could tell, her body was perfect as it was.

She wagged her spoon. "Nope. Two more pounds turns to five more in a heartbeat, and if I gain five pounds then I have to start jogging or something just to get it off. It's easier to catch it now."

"There's nothing wrong with jogging."

"Spoken like a man who lives where the land is relatively flat," she teased.

Lucky breathed a sigh of relief. It looked as if Annie was going to ignore what had happened early this morning. Maybe she was one of those rare women who could enjoy sex for the sake of sex. He hadn't pegged her as the type, but anything was possible. He'd been wrong about the tattoo, after all.

Of course, she hadn't looked directly at him since she'd entered the kitchen. Maybe she was intent on her breakfast, since she was hungry, but then again—maybe she was simply *pretending* that what had happened meant nothing. Annie had never struck him as the sneaky type.

Since she wasn't looking at him, he felt free to stare. Something about the feminine curve of her cheek and the swell beneath that snug shirt grabbed him and wouldn't let go. His body responded. He wanted her again. Maybe on that table where she was finishing up her yogurt, maybe in the shower, or on the couch, or…

Crap. Lucky turned around and left the kitchen before Annie had the chance to look his way and see what she'd done to him. Sleeping with a woman once could be brushed aside as casual and unimportant.

Wanting her all the time would only lead to disaster, for him, and for her.

He needed to get closer. Not into the house; not yet. It was too soon for him to visit and to touch. But he wanted to get close enough to hear their voices, to smell them. Watching from such a distance was no longer satisfying in any but the smallest way.

Creeping through the woods, he made his way toward the house he'd been watching for over a week. It was broad daylight, but even if anyone saw him they wouldn't think him out of place. He was a common sight in and around Mercerville these days, and if anyone questioned him he'd have a believable story to tell. He always did.

Without making a sound, he made his way to the house until he could touch the exterior wall. *She* was still in there; *he* was gone. What would she say if he went to the door and knocked? She'd invite him inside, of course. She'd offer him iced tea and maybe cookies.

But it was too soon for that. He made his way to the back of the house and the small, low door there. It opened slowly and soundlessly, and he slipped into the crawl space and closed the door behind him.

He turned on a small flashlight and oriented himself to the space. It was adequate. More than adequate, in fact.

He had to stoop down to walk in the crawl space, and the floor was packed dirt and cold stone. A few old tools that looked as if they hadn't been used in years were stored here. A rusty hacksaw. A square-head shovel, also rusty. The better tools were stored in a fairly new shed in the backyard.

The backpack he wore contained everything he'd need. A blanket, to carpet the ground. A dim flashlight. Water. Granola bars, in case he got hungry. He took a moment to prepare the space, and then he lay down upon the blanket and turned off his flashlight.

The house was old, and in some spaces light from the house shone down, slanting between old, loose floorboards. He'd have to be very, very quiet, so no one would ever know he was here. He closed his eyes and listened. Her footsteps sounded soft above him. A radio played in the background. Country music. He liked country music.

Sometimes she hummed along with the music, if the song was familiar. She was cleaning, he guessed after a few moments of listening. She moved from room to room, and he heard the swish of a broom and the quick spray of cleaner or furniture polish. He liked that, that she kept her house so clean. She was a caring woman, a good woman.

The phone rang, jarring him so that his eyes flew open. She answered. "Hello?"

He listened to the one-sided conversation, and it didn't take him long to realize that *he* was calling.

"I could use a gallon of milk and some diet soda, if you don't mind."

All was quiet for a moment, but for the country music in the background, and then she laughed. What had he said that was funny? It was annoying not to know, but it couldn't be helped. Tonight, when the workday was done and they were both here, he'd be able to hear both sides of the conversation.

She finished the phone call with a sincere "Love you, too," and then returned to her chores.

For a few minutes the man beneath the house remained very still. Love. It was the most powerful force in the universe, and it had once been his. That time was gone. Now he was forced to experience love through others, because he could never know it again. Never, never, never. Love remained elusive, just out of reach. Maybe this couple would help him to understand what love was, and then he could make *her* understand, and then he could be happy again.

He hadn't been happy for such a very long time.

Above his head the woman began to hum again. Fittingly, it was a song about lost love.

All day long, she'd felt as if her skin was on fire. For days, Lucky had been putting his arm around her, taking her hand, smiling at her. She knew it was all for show, but now everything felt different. What had happened in his bed had not been for show. It had been just for them.

For her, everything was different. For Lucky, nothing had changed.

His focus was all about finding the killer. They'd done their thing in town, holding hands and smiling and acting like blissfully content lovers, hoping to draw attention. He'd made phone calls and taken notes and made more phone calls. That was as it should be, right? She'd brought him here to stop a murderer—and her dreams. The fabulous sex was just a bonus.

Or the biggest mistake of her life.

It would be best to pretend that nothing had happened. She'd say good night, go to bed, lock her door and sleep alone. Lucky would continue to pretend that nothing had changed, and she'd pretend that taking a man into her bed could be in any way casual.

Annie liked trendy clothes and popular music. She was, in most ways, a thoroughly modern woman. But when it came to sex, she couldn't get rid of the notion that to invite a man into your bed and your body was important. It was no wonder that until this morning she hadn't slept with a man in five years.

It was a cool night, so a few hours ago, right after supper, Lucky had built a fire in the fireplace. He'd fed it now and again, carefully adding firewood when the flames grew too small. It was getting late now, and he was allowing the fire to die down.

Their conversation had been all about the case, primarily about how it was not going well. His inquiries had revealed nothing of importance, though there were Benning agents and law-enforcement friends continuing to investigate.

An Important Message from the Editors

Dear Reader,

If you'd enjoy reading romance novels with larger print that's easier on your eyes, let us send you TWO FREE HARLEQUIN INTRIGUE® NOVELS in our NEW LARGER PRINT EDITION. These books are complete and unabridged, but the type is set about 20% bigger to make it easier to read. Look inside for an actual-size sample.

By the way, you'll also get a surprise gift with your two free books!

Pam Powers

Peel off Seal and Place Inside...

THE RIGHT WOMAN

she'd thought she was fine. It took Daniel's words and Brooke's question to make her realize she was far from a full recovery.

She'd made a start with her sister's help and she intended to go forward now. Sarah felt as if she'd been living in a darkened room and some-one had suddenly opened a door, letting in the fresh air and sunshine. She could feel its warmth slowly seeping into the coldest part of her. The feeling was liberating. She realized it was only a small step and she had a long way to go, but she was ready to face life again with Serena and her family behind her.

All too soon, they were saying goodbye and Sarah experienced a moment of sadness for all the years she and Serena had missed. But they had each other now, and that's what ...

She held ...

PRINTED IN THE U.S.A.
Publisher acknowledges the copyright holder of the excerpt from this individual work as follows:
THE RIGHT WOMAN Copyright © 2004 by Linda Warren. All rights reserved.
® and TM are trademarks owned and used by the trademark owner and/or its licensee

YOURS FREE!
You'll get a great mystery gift with your two free larger print books!

GET TWO FREE LARGER PRINT BOOKS!

YES! Please send me two free Harlequin Intrigue® romantic suspense novels in the larger print edition, and my free mystery gift, too. I understand that I am under no obligation to purchase anything, as explained on the back of this insert.

PLACE FREE GIFTS SEAL HERE

199 HDL EE44   399 HDL EE5G

FIRST NAME   LAST NAME

ADDRESS

APT.#   CITY

STATE/PROV.   ZIP/POSTAL CODE

Are you a current Harlequin Intrigue® subscriber and want to receive the larger print edition?
Call 1-800-221-5011 today!

▼ DETACH AND MAIL CARD TODAY! ▼

(H-ILPS-09/06) © 2004 Harlequin Enterprises Ltd.

The Harlequin Reader Service™ — Here's How It Works:

Accepting your 2 free Harlequin Intrigue® larger print books and gift places you under no obligation to buy anything. You may keep the books and gift and return the shipping statement marked "cancel." If you do not cancel, about a month later we'll send you 6 additional Harlequin Intrigue larger print books and bill you just $4.49 each in the U.S., or $5.24 each in Canada, plus 25¢ shipping & handling per book and applicable taxes if any.* That's the complete price and — compared to cover prices of $5.25 each in the U.S. and $6.25 each in Canada — it's quite a bargain! You may cancel at any time, but if you choose to continue, every month we'll send you 6 more books, which you may either purchase at the discount price or return to us and cancel your subscription.

*Terms and prices subject to change without notice. Sales tax applicable in N.Y. Canadian residents will be charged applicable provincial taxes and GST.

If offer card is missing write to: Harlequin Reader Service, 3010 Walden Ave., P.O. Box 1867, Buffalo, NY 14240-1867

BUSINESS REPLY MAIL
FIRST-CLASS MAIL   PERMIT NO. 717-003   BUFFALO, NY

POSTAGE WILL BE PAID BY ADDRESSEE

HARLEQUIN READER SERVICE
3010 WALDEN AVE
PO BOX 1867
BUFFALO NY 14240-9952

NO POSTAGE
NECESSARY
IF MAILED
IN THE
UNITED STATES

"So, anything?" he asked abruptly, glancing her way and—for the first time all evening—looking her in the eye.

Annie shook her head. He'd been asking her all day about tapping into the killer's brain, but no matter how hard she tried to reach beyond the small circle of her life, all she could see was Lucky. She couldn't get away from his fear that she'd expect more than he had to give. His horror that she might cling. His absolute terror that a woman, any woman, might need him in anything more than the most superficial of ways.

Making love to him had meant everything to her, but to Lucky it had meant less than nothing. Even though her body wanted his, and it would be so very easy to give him what he wanted without asking for more than he cared to give, she couldn't.

Annie curled up on her chair, and looked at Lucky with all the fearlessness she could muster. "I need more," she said simply.

For a moment he was silent and confused, and then he realized that she'd once again changed the subject without warning. "Sorry."

"I'm not," she said clearly.

When she allowed her mind to reach out she could see into his so clearly. It was frightening, and if he knew…if he knew how well she connected to him now, he would run for the hills, killer or no killer.

He liked her well enough; he wanted her fiercely; he was terrified of her. He was terrified she'd get too close and make him feel something he couldn't handle.

There was another woman, from long ago, someone who'd hurt him so badly he had not yet recovered. The truth was, he might never recover. Lucky Santana was not the best at letting things go.

"It's not like what we've been pretending is in any way real," she said. "We have to remember that. This morning, I allowed myself to forget." She shrugged her shoulders slightly. "I was scared and you were there, and you were…" *Horny* sounded so crude, even though it was true. "You were willing enough, so it's not like anyone got hurt."

If she let him get any closer, he'd break her heart when he left. And he was going to leave. As it was, she could watch him walk away when the time came without being destroyed. She was fond of him, and she would always remember what it had felt like when he'd made love to her, but soon enough she'd forget him and get on with her life.

And there it was…the mental image of Lucky above her, the fan whirring, the scar. Last night they had not been in her bed, but in his. She'd thought maybe that was just an aberration, but the vision of what was to come remained with her. She had no sense of time, where that vision was concerned. Would he make love to her in that bed in a day? A week? A year?

No, she wasn't sure when the vision would come to pass, but she did know it wouldn't happen tonight.

Why did she see that vision so clearly, when she hadn't seen their first time together at all? What was it about that particular instance that was so important she'd seen it the first time she'd touched Lucky?

Maybe what she experienced—then and now—was

simply a wish, not a vision at all. Just because she knew Lucky Santana was bad for her and her sentimental heart, that didn't mean she didn't want him.

Chapter 9

It was going on two in the morning, sleep was elusive and Lucky felt like a jerk. Maybe he was. It wouldn't be the first time.

He also felt as if he'd lost something, and that was foolish. He barely knew Annie Lockhart, so how could he have lost her? A little distance was best. A lot would be better.

Still, after she went to bed he found himself e-mailing Murphy with a few requests. He hadn't planned to be here so long, and he needed some supplies. Besides, he was damned tired of Annie telling him he dressed like her father.

If they'd attracted the attention of the man they were looking for, Annie hadn't picked up on it yet. He had a feeling she would know when, and if, that happened—if it was possible. If her gift was as real as it seemed to be. If he hadn't let a pretty woman hoodwink him.

Now and then he wondered if maybe he'd allowed himself to be snookered. Maybe Annie didn't have any psychic ability. Of course, that didn't necessarily mean she'd conned him. Maybe he'd spent the past week chasing after a boogeyman from a too-vivid nightmare and she truly believed her boogeyman was real. He'd been suckered into this because Annie was pretty and feminine, and she had big blue eyes that drew him in. She had the ability to look lost and vulnerable. It was his weakness, after all, this need to save the girl.

"Sir Freakin' Lucky," he mumbled beneath his breath as he sent the e-mail.

It was after three before he went to bed. Sleep was a while longer coming. The sheets smelled of her. The room smelled of Annie and sex and something else he couldn't identify, as if she'd left a part of herself here. She was sleeping just down the hall, and when he thought of her lying in her bed, so near, he got hard again.

Great. Just great.

He finally slept, and when he did he dreamed of Annie. He woke just after seven to the mechanical ring of his cell phone. None too happy to be disturbed, he answered with a bark. "Santana. This better be good."

The last person he expected to find on the other end of the call was Truman McCain. The last thing he expected hear was "We're headed your way. We'll be there early this afternoon."

* * *

Annie busied herself with a new design—brightly colored sequined fish on a black-and-gold handbag—while Lucky buried himself in paperwork he'd gone over a hundred times. He seemed to think if he organized his notes in another way he'd see something he'd missed before. Anything to keep them from actually talking to one another.

Sadie was coming. *The* Sadie. The one Lucky thought himself in love with—or had. Annie knew he didn't love the woman who had once been his partner, but did he think it was true?

Yes. He did.

She never should've slept with Lucky. Since that final, heart-stopping moment when they'd come together, it was as if she could slip into his mind at will, and with amazing ease. In the past, seeing into another's mind had always been jarring and uncomfortable and even frightening. But this was very natural and comforting. It made a kind of sense, she supposed. He'd suggested that physical proximity played a part in her ability. What closer physical proximity was possible than what she and Lucky had shared?

This hadn't happened with Seth, though. Not even close. She hadn't had a clue that he would bolt when she began to dream of the murder in Nashville. But of course, he hadn't touched her after the ability kicked into gear so…

It was just too complicated. Making hats and handbags was easier, and she did her best to lose herself in that activity.

After a while, the silence got to be too much. "I could call Kristie and cancel dinner tonight, if you think it's best."

"No," Lucky said, giving her half of his attention— if that much. "Sadie and Truman McCain will be long gone by suppertime. She won't leave the kids with her mother-in-law overnight."

"Doesn't trust her?"

"I don't know," Lucky grumbled. "It's some mother thing, I guess."

Some mother thing. He growled the words as if he didn't understand them at all. And in truth, he didn't. Annie tried very hard not to peek where she shouldn't, but when it came to Lucky's own mother, it was difficult not to see. No wonder he was so messed up where women were concerned. Not hopelessly messed up, she was coming to understand, but still...definitely off-kilter.

"I don't suppose you've started on my order yet," he asked without looking at her.

"The diaper bag with the built-in holster?" She laughed. "No."

"Don't wait until the kid's out of diapers."

Annie set her work aside and watched Lucky. He was sorting out some kind of file on his laptop, and his eyes were glued to the computer screen. "I can't believe you're serious about that."

"I'm serious."

"A diaper bag with a place for a gun...."

"Did you question the woman who ordered that hat I saw you wearing last week the way you're questioning me?" he asked sharply, lifting his head to look at her for a brief moment.

"No, but…I tell you what. We'll ask Sadie what she thinks, when she gets here. If she thinks it's a great idea, I'll get to work on the bag immediately and I won't charge you a dime. If she thinks it's as ridiculous an idea as I do, then you have to order something else. Something very expensive and not at all related to firearms."

"Fine," he said absently. "I wanted to surprise her, but if that's the way you want to play this, you'd better get busy. Once she knows about the plan, I'm sure she'll want the bag right away."

The day passed too slowly, in that way they did when anticipation filled the air. Since she had already decided that there was nothing of substance between her and Lucky, she shouldn't be anxious about meeting the woman he had once thought himself in love with. And still, she wondered how she compared to the fabulous Sadie.

Thanks to her newfound insight, she knew Lucky wanted her. Physically, at least. What did that mean? Not much. She'd reached him in an entirely sexual way, but what about his heart? Would she, or anyone else, ever reach that deeply inside him?

The alarm that had been installed at the foot of the long driveway sounded, and Lucky finished what he was doing and closed his laptop. He glanced at the monitor near his computer, saw a familiar vehicle making the approach and nodded. "It's them."

Annie put away her supplies. Her heart beat hard. Sadie was here. The Sadie who had touched Lucky's heart in a way no other woman ever had. Perfect Sadie, with whom she could not hope to compete.

Car doors slammed shut, and from outside the cabin they heard a man's voice. And then in answer a child's voice.

Lucky snapped a curse word and snatched up his laptop. "Truman said they were leaving the kids with his mother, but there must've been a change of plans. Hide anything breakable." He moved the monitors and alarms, along with his laptop, to the top of her bookshelf. He pointed to the sofa. "Scissors. Get those out of here if you value anything you own."

Annie smiled as she picked up the scissors and stuck them high on the bookshelf. "It can't be that bad."

"You've never met Grant."

A few moments later, she did. The McCains didn't enter the cabin, they exploded into it. Grant rushed to Lucky and threw himself at the man he called Unca Lucky. The baby spit up on her father as they walked through the front door, and no one seemed concerned or surprised. Sadie and her husband were both explaining—simultaneously—why they'd had to bring the kids with them. Apparently Grandma had awakened with all the signs of a cold, and they didn't want to take the chance that the germs might spread to the kids. The only thing worse than taking care of two kids was taking care of two sick kids.

Lucky made quick introductions amidst the pandemonium. Sadie and Truman both nodded and smiled, and Grant tossed her a very enthusiastic "Hello!" Reagan just cooed, and then she spit up again. When that was done, Annie stepped back and observed. Her usually serene cabin was in chaos, noisy and crowded and practically shaking—especially when Grant vaulted from Lucky's arms onto the couch and then to the floor.

Sadie got a hug from her old partner; Truman got a handshake. And then Sadie handed the baby to a horrified Lucky.

Annie smiled as she watched the reunion. Of course Lucky loved Sadie. She was his family. She and her husband and their kids were the closest thing he'd ever known to true, loving kin, but he didn't recognize it as such. He just knew he needed them, and he didn't like even that.

What Lucky felt for Sadie wasn't romantic love and never had been, but she had become a big part of the loving family he had never known.

So many pieces of the puzzle fell together as she watched, and she wanted to wrap her arms around Lucky's neck, hold him close and tell him that she understood. She wanted to be in his bed again, or invite him into hers. She wanted to love him without restraint or worry about what tomorrow might bring.

Lucky Santana did have a heart, but he protected it so staunchly it was almost unreachable. *Almost.*

Truman McCain had a minor limp, and Annie knew without reaching that it wasn't a sprained ankle or such but an old injury that pained him. He didn't think surgery could help, but in a few years—a very few—a procedure to repair the damage there would all but end that telling limp and the pain that still visited too often. It was so obvious that the sheriff and his wife loved one another, that Annie felt an envy that had nothing to do with Lucky. What they had was rare and beautiful. At least they had the good sense to appreciate what they'd found.

Within twenty minutes of their arrival, an exhausted Grant fell asleep on the sofa. Reagan fell asleep in the crook of her father's arm. Sadie and Lucky retrieved two suitcases, which they said Murphy had delivered at the crack of dawn after finding out via Sadie's e-mail that they were making the trip to Tennessee.

The suitcases were stored in Lucky's room, and with the kids asleep and the cabin relatively quiet once again, Sadie spread a large map of the southeastern United States across the dining room table. Someone had made several markings across the state of Georgia and into Tennessee.

"First of all, this isn't complete," Truman said. "I have inquiries out and it might be weeks before I hear back from everyone. It would be impossible to investigate the entire country, so I limited my inquiries to the Southeast, at least for now. What I've found so far is enough to get me here." He glanced at Annie with suspicion. "I have to tell you, I'm not a believer in things I can't see, but I do agree that the Huffs' deaths are suspicious and warrant a decent in-vestigation. Now that I've seen the facts, I can't let it go."

"I appreciate your honesty."

He pointed to the map, one finger landing on a red mark south of Atlanta. "These might not all be related, but they're all suspicious. The odds are most of these are exactly what they appear to be. Accidents, domestic crimes, robberies that ended in violence."

Annie studied the red-dotted map, and her stomach flipped unpleasantly. "All of these dots represent death?"

"Every one represents a couple who died in a way that someone thought was suspicious. Home invasion," Sadie said, pointing to another small red dot. "Even though the house was small and there was nothing of value to take." Her finger moved up. "A couple killed coming out of a movie theater. The killer took their wedding rings. Nothing else."

Truman pointed to a small town in north Georgia. "Murder/suicide, much like the one that took place here. This is going to take time, but all I can do is look at the facts of each case and see if anything jumps out at me. If we can come up with another murder and tie it to the one here, then we can get the FBI involved. We might also be able to come up with a time line which will help us assemble a list of suspects. If he was here two years ago—" one finger found a random red dot on the map "—then he wasn't in Mercerville."

Sadie looked at Annie. "It's been nearly three months since the Huffs were killed, and according to Lucky he's already chosen his next set of victims."

"I know." Annie's knees went weak, and even though she tried very hard to hide that reaction, Lucky was soon there. He placed an arm around her waist and supported her, in a way that would look casual to Sadie and Truman, but which offered Annie real support.

"Odds are, that means he's new to the area. If he moves from victim to victim so quickly, then it's likely he hasn't been a resident of Mercerville very long. Considering the MO, I'd say he killed once or twice, likely in different ways each time, and then, before things get too hot, he moves on to another town and another couple."

"I guess you called Larkin with this," Lucky said. He didn't sound happy about the prospect.

"Not yet," Sadie answered. "Until we actually have a list of suspicious crimes that we can link to this one, what's he going to do? Max is too fond of overkill. He'd send a dozen federal agents in and the killer would bolt. Unless you have an objection, we thought maybe we'd wait until we have more concrete evidence."

"We?" Lucky grinned. "I thought you were retired."

"Semiretired," Sadie argued. "As long as I do my part on the computer or over the phone, Truman doesn't mind."

It looked to Annie as if Truman did mind, but he knew his wife well enough to know she'd never be the Suzy Homemaker type.

"This information could've been shared by e-mail or phone," Lucky said. "Why the in-person visit?"

"Complaining?" Sadie asked.

"No. Just curious."

Her eyes cut away from him and she pretended to study the cabin's furnishings. "It's a pretty time of year up this way. We thought we'd take in the changing leaves."

Lucky snorted. "I don't get the whole leaf obsession."

"Besides, I heard from Murphy late last night, and he said you'd asked him to send up some stuff."

"Hasn't he ever heard of FedEx?"

Sadie glanced at Annie. The mother of two had been just as curious about the woman Lucky was working for as Annie had been about her. What had Murphy said to make her so curious?

"Lucky has placed a special order for you and the new baby," Annie said, anxious to change to subject—even if just for a moment. "He wants me to make a pink diaper bag with a special compartment for a gun."

She waited for laughter and shouts of horror. Sadie's mouth opened slightly, and then she looked at Lucky and grinned. Truman shook his head and grumbled. Annie grinned, glad of the win—however small.

And then Sadie laughed out loud. "Lucky, that's perfect!"

Truman had vetoed the diaper bag idea, so after the McCains left, Lucky and Annie declared a draw where Reagan's gift was concerned, and set the subject aside. They had bigger concerns, now that Truman and Sadie had suggested that there might be an experienced serial killer in their midst. Once a few more facts were in place it would be easy to get the sheriff's department, the state and the federal government involved. All afternoon Sadie had been working on a list of the newest residents of the area. Not only Mercerville, but out in the county, as well. She didn't know everyone, but it was a start.

The new postman. The guy who'd bought the fudge shop in late spring. A plumber who'd joined a local company just four months back. A carpenter who did odd jobs. There were others who had been in the area less than a year, but most of them had come with wives, or larger families. Annie wasn't sure, but she suspected the killer was a solitary man. She'd sensed a deep loneliness in him, a longing for loving connections that he didn't have.

Kristie and Stu Bentley were also newer to Mercer-ville than Lucky had suspected. They'd bought the bed-and-breakfast five months ago, and according to what they'd told Annie, they'd been married less than a year. Was it possible they were looking for a duo of killers, or that Stu had not only his neighbors but his wife fooled?

Lucky was tempted to cancel supper with the Bentleys, even though Sadie and Truman had been gone for a couple of hours and time was not an issue. Three reasons spurred him onward. He and Annie had an appearance to maintain, even though with any luck the end of the investigation was near. Secondly, a few more hours alone in this cabin with Annie and he was going to explode.

And lastly, in his mind the Bentleys were now suspects. Annie dismissed the idea as ludicrous, but until he knew better, Lucky wasn't about to strike them from the list. They'd been in the park that afternoon when Annie had felt the killer was near.

No matter how nice and normal the Bentleys appeared to be, anything was possible. Anything at all.

Annie grinned at him when he stepped into the main room of her cabin. "Nice," she said. "Where'd you get the duds?"

"They're undercover duds." Faded black jeans, mo-torcycle boots, a Harley T-shirt. He did own more than nicely tailored and expensive suits, and much of it was stored at Benning's main offices—just in case. What she couldn't see was the perfectly fitted ankle holster that had been made for these boots, and the small revolver that was housed there.

Annie's grin faded slowly. "I never would've thought it, but I miss the suit. As nice as this look is, it just isn't…you."

She, of course, was dressed in her usual off-the-wall garb. The skirt was full and colorful and hung well below her knees, where they met a dark brown pair of boots not all that different from his black ones. Her T-shirt was decorated with sparkly things; the bracelet and dangly earrings she wore looked as if they'd been made to match. Given her profession, that was entirely possible.

Lucky leaned against the doorway and studied her from head to toe. "Why on earth would a beautiful woman get all dressed up and finish off the outfit with clunky boots?"

Annie rocked back on her heels. "If I ever see a beautiful woman wearing clunky boots, I'll ask her."

She wasn't teasing him, he could tell. She was putting him in his place. Telling him not to bullshit her. Drawing a line and daring him to cross it. How could she not know she was beautiful? There had been a time when he'd thought her pretty, not gorgeous, but that had changed in the past few days. If Annie walked into a room packed with women, he'd notice her to the exclusion of all others.

Crap. He still wanted her, and at the moment no other woman would do. He suspected that feeling would vanish as soon as the job was done, but right now it was unexpectedly powerful.

He crossed the room slowly, the heels of his boots thudding against the wooden floor. He went directly to Annie, tipped her chin up and said it again, in a low, steady voice. "Why would a beautiful woman like you wear such clunky boots?"

There was no smile, now. Annie swallowed, nervous to have him so close even though he'd been closer—and would be again, he suspected, in spite of his insistence that whatever relationship they had was over. He felt Annie's gentle tremble in the fingers that remained at her chin. Yes, he would definitely be *close* to her again.

"I'm not beautiful," she argued. "When I work at it, I can be cute, and I'm always fashionable, but that's about as far as it goes. I know my limitations, Lucky. You've spent your entire adult life in the company of gorgeous women who could be models or movie stars. I'm ordinary. Not ugly, but certainly not beautiful."

"Since you've just declared me an expert, shouldn't that be up to me to decide?"

"No," she argued weakly.

He kissed her, because she was so close and because he could. Because her lips were full and inviting and right *there*. Because he wanted her.

This was going to be the longest night of his life. Why hadn't he called off dinner and arranged surveillance of the B and B down the hill? He could have any number of Benning agents here within a few hours, and they could take over the investigation while he looked out for Annie. Besides, he had no desire to spend time with perky Kristie and her too-quiet husband.

"Don't be silly," Annie said as she ended the kiss. "You'll like Kristie and Stu once you get to know them. Everything will be fine." All of a sudden, she went very still. Her body stiffened. "You didn't say that out loud, did you?"

"No, I didn't." Dammit, Annie was peeking into his

head again, and he didn't like it. He also didn't like the fact that it came so easily to her, that it had taken her a moment to realize that he hadn't actually voiced his thoughts aloud.

"Well, I'm sorry if you don't like it, but that's just the way it is," she said defensively. "If you don't want me peeking into your head, then…think of baseball."

She blushed, then turned around swiftly and snatched a colorful handbag from the sofa.

Great. If she could see into his head so clearly and easily, then she knew he wanted her. Not that he cared that she knew. They were two unattached adults who'd had dynamite sex and did not want that one eventful morning to be the end of it.

Whether she'd admit it or not, Annie still wanted him, and he didn't have to be psychic to know it. All it had taken to confirm the suspicion was that one telling kiss.

Chapter 10

Behind the bed-and-breakfast where guests slept in antique beds and ate in a dining room that could easily accommodate twenty sat a much smaller house where Kristie and Stu Bentley lived. Kristie spent much of her time in the bed-and-breakfast, cooking, cleaning and playing hostess to her guests, but this much smaller carriage house was home to her and her husband. The décor throughout was a bit more modern, and the dining room was just right for four people. The small, round oak table would be crowded with six diners, and impossible with eight.

All through dinner at that oak table, Annie felt as if someone was watching her. Goose bumps rose up on her arms, and the back of her neck tingled. Kristie was a great cook, but the food tasted like cardboard in her mouth. Even Lucky in his undercover duds couldn't distract her enough to dismiss the odd sensation of being under constant observation. When Kristie reached for the rolls and knocked over her glass of iced tea, Annie jumped out of her chair as if she'd heard a gunshot, even though the spilled tea didn't come anywhere near her.

Her heart pounded. If Lucky wasn't sitting next to her, cool as could be, she'd probably run from the house screaming. Was it possible that he was right in naming Stu a suspect? While she couldn't put her finger on the sensations that flitted and jumped through her body, she did feel like the killer was watching her closely.

If it was Stu—and she wasn't ready to accept that it could be—then Kristie was entirely innocent. Poor thing, she'd need the support of her friends, if it turned out that her new husband was a murderer. Annie wracked her brain to remember every word Kristie had said about Stu. They hadn't known one another for a very long time, she did remember that. Kristie said she'd been swept off her feet by Stu, who in Annie's opinion was not the sweeping type. Lucky, on the other hand…

If Lucky sensed that anything was wrong, you'd never know it from the way he acted. All through dinner he and Stu talked about football and baseball and—to her surprise—lawn care. She wouldn't have expected Lucky to know anything about different types of grass and fertilizer, but he did. She knew he had a house, but she'd always suspected he hired out all his yardwork. Maybe not. Maybe she didn't know everything about him, after all.

He was very good at hiding his feelings. If he still suspected Stu Bentley of being the man who'd murdered the Huffs, no one would ever know it.

Now and then Lucky took her hand beneath the table and gently squeezed in a gesture of support and comfort. Unlike him, she was a total failure at hiding how she felt. Lucky knew she was nervous.

He likely *didn't* know she felt as if the man who'd invaded her dreams with his violence was close. Very close.

After supper, they sat in the den and visited for a while. The house was quiet, and Kristie didn't have to run over to the main house as she did most evenings, since the group staying at the bed-and-breakfast was not yet back from their day trip to Gatlinburg. Kristie had the energy of a hummingbird. There were always a few guests in the bed-and-breakfast, and at certain times of the year it was filled to capacity. And on a rare evening off, she chose to entertain. Did she ever sit still for more than a few minutes? Lucky was right; Kristie *was* perky.

Eventually, Lucky stood and told their host and hostess that it was getting late and they needed to go. Even though Annie adored Kristie and usually loved spending time with her and her husband, she'd never been so grateful to get out of any place. When she left this carriage house, would she also leave behind the sensation of being under a microscope?

Guilt didn't help matters any. Kristie was her friend, and she felt as if she were betraying that friendship by bringing Lucky here to spy, to observe Annie's friends as if they were specimens under a microscope.

But if Stu was the killer…

Lucky held her hand as they stepped onto the front porch. The gesture wasn't entirely for show. His car was parked in the narrow gravel driveway, very close to the wide covered porch. Dark shadows surrounded the house, beyond the small circle of light the front porch lamps cast. Not too far away, the warm, welcoming lights of the bed-and-breakfast shone, so out of place in the modern world, it was almost surreal. Lace curtains draped perfectly in the windows, and the mellow light that shone through the narrow old panes came, in some instances, from antique lamps. In many of the windows, antique figurines sat on wide window-sills.

Beyond the rear porch of the main house there were more shadows, shadows that were deep and unfathomable. Was the person she felt watching out there? Or standing right behind her? She didn't know, not with any certainty. The phone rang, and Kristie rushed to answer. Stu said good-night and closed the door.

Instead of hurrying them to his car, Lucky sat on the front step and pulled Annie down to sit beside him. His arm went around her, natural and easy and very welcomed, and he pulled her close.

"What the hell is wrong?" he whispered.

She shook her head. Not here. Not here where some-one—like Stu—might hear.

He touched one wayward lock of her hair and let his fingers linger. "I've never known anyone like you, Annie Lockhart, and I'm not just talking about the obvious oddities."

She knew what he was talking about—her psychic abilities—but still, *oddities?* "Gee, thanks."

He studied her for a long moment, and then he took her hand. It was a gesture of comfort, she knew, even though Lucky wasn't the type of man who normally offered comfort. He was a "get over it" kinda guy, where problems were concerned. If he couldn't shoot at it or capture it, then he didn't think there was anything else he could do to help. But right now, when all her problems were on the inside, he was pretty good at the comforting thing.

He might never say so, but he did care about her.

"There are a couple of things I should tell you about me," he said, brushing his thumb across the palm of her hand. "Do I have any secrets left where you're concerned?"

"A few," she answered honestly.

"I suppose I should be grateful for that much." He sounded like he was teasing, but Lucky never teased, right?

"What is it that you want to tell me?" she asked.

Instead of answering right away he kissed her, and she opened her lips to him, gratefully and hungrily. And while he kissed her, the sensation of being watched faded. Lucky had the power to push whatever unnatural abilities she possessed deep, so that they weren't resting so closely, so fragile, just under the skin. At the moment the only thing under her skin was Lucky Santana.

She liked it.

He lay beneath the house on the cool ground, very still, hardly breathing. Maybe it had been foolish to choose to watch a couple who lived near a public house that was so often busy. People came and went at all hours. In a way that only added to the excitement of watching and listening, but the traffic in and out of the bed-and-breakfast also made it very difficult to plan his next move.

Tonight, the visiting couple had stolen his interest. Next to Annie Lockhart and the man she'd taken up with, the Bentleys paled. They seemed ordinary, even dull.

Instead of remaining in place and listening to *her* talk on the phone while *he* began to gather dirty dishes, he scooted toward the front porch, moving very slowly and without making a sound. Annie and her boyfriend were still there, and they were talking in hushed tones.

He'd seen them around town over the past week. They were an odd couple, obviously drawn together by sexual attraction. Santana was a bit of a brute, even when he wore a suit that was apparently supposed to make him look more respectable. Maybe his obvious mixed blood had given him an inferiority complex. No amount of window dressing could make Santana look like anything less than the brute he was.

The man hiding beneath the house wasn't really interested in sexual attraction. It was explosive, especially in the early stages of a relationship, but sex didn't last. Not like true love. In a few days or a few weeks, Santana would be gone. He didn't belong here; he didn't belong with Annie.

When he'd moved as far as he could toward the front porch, which wasn't all the way thanks to a slope of the land beneath him, he stopped and strained to listen.

They were still there. Kissing, judging by the soft sounds that drifted his way.

He closed his eyes, and listened hard. The kiss went on for a while, and then it was followed by a feminine sigh.

"How do you do it?" Annie asked. "I swear, there are moments when you make everything else go away."

"Everything?"

"Everything."

Annie made a sound that might've been a soft, half laugh. It was hard to tell, without seeing her face. "I can't believe I miss the suit."

Santana's answer was a soft growl. "I can't believe I'm starting to think those army boots are sexy. Maybe it's because I know under there the toenails are red. Very sexy stuff, hiding something so feminine under boots that look as if they belong in my closet, not yours."

The porch creaked as they stood, and then they kissed again.

He remembered what it was like to be so in love, it was impossible to keep his hands off of the woman he loved. He remembered what it was like to kiss, and kiss again. That comment Annie had made about making everything go away, it was very romantic.

Maybe there was love here, after all.

For a moment he was distracted. True, Santana was big and would put up quite a fight, if the opportunity arose, but then again, with the proper drugs in his system he wouldn't be able to fight at all. He'd be manageable enough. And as for Annie, she was just a little slip of a thing, and by the time she thought to put up a struggle, it would be too late.

From the house above, soft laughter sounded. It rolled and grew and filled the crawl space where he hid with warmth. He dismissed Annie and Santana, as they walked away from the house. Maybe they were in love, maybe one day he'd choose to watch them and share in that love, for a while.

But for now, Kristie and Stu filled the void that made him feel so empty and lost. They would continue to complete him, they would continue to fill that void until they disappointed him. When that happened, he'd make them pay.

Of course, it was always possible that the Bentleys wouldn't disappoint him, that they would continue to bring happiness to his sad life for many years to come. He was happy here, lying on the packed earth listening to them laugh and share the details of their day.

In the end they all disappointed him, but he had hope that Stu and Kristie would be different. And if they were like all the rest, well, then maybe he'd turn his attentions to Annie and Santana.

Lucky set the alarms he'd installed, as soon as they were in the cabin with the door closed behind them. There were not only alarms on every door and window, but on the driveway, and along the perimeter of her property. She wasn't convinced that the killer would ever turn his attentions their way, but if he did, he wouldn't get close without Lucky knowing he was here.

While he tended to the alarms, she built a small fire in the fireplace. He'd stacked wood nearby that afternoon, so they could have a fire without fetching logs from the woodpile after dark. With a starter log and lots of kindling the fire was blazing in no time.

She sat on the sofa and watched the flames, and a moment later Lucky joined her. His arm went casually and comfortably around her.

"Better?" he asked softly.

"Yes."

"Want to tell me why you were so antsy tonight?"

She shuddered. "I felt like I was being watched all night. Maybe I just felt that way because you added Stu to the list of suspects, and he was right there and I hate lying to Kristie about everything. You, the Huffs, your suspicions…my visions."

"You can't keep hiding them, you know."

"They'll go away once you catch the guy," she insisted.

"What if they don't?" He gently forced her to look him in the eye. "What if this time they stay?"

Annie sighed. "I don't want to be a freak. I just want…"

"What do you want, Annie?"

I want you to love me. She was very glad, at that moment, that Lucky couldn't read her mind. A confession like that would send him running.

"I want you to hold me."

That was one request he didn't mind agreeing to. He did as she asked; he took her in his arms and held her. Why was it that Lucky had the ability to chase away all these things that frightened her? Visions, loneliness, the feeling that no one would ever want her the way she wanted him at this moment.

"I can't stay," he said, his fingers in her hair and his

body so close to hers, she could almost drink in his body heat and his heartbeat.

"I know. But you're here now, and maybe that's enough." She still wasn't into casual sex, but what if she never again felt this way? What if Lucky was her one shot at the real thing, and she sent him on his way because he couldn't offer her forever?

"Maybe," he said, pulling the one uncertain word from her sentence and throwing it back at her. Gently, of course.

Annie laid her lips on Lucky's neck and kissed, allowing her mouth to linger so she could taste his skin. She sucked gently, drawing in his scent. Wonderfully, amazingly, she didn't think of anything else but the way her body reached for his, the way her heart beat too fast when he held her.

She ran her hand up his thigh and traced the length of his zipper with her fingernails. Beneath the worn black jeans he was hard. Ready. Her palm settled over him and she took a deep breath before looking him squarely in the eye. "You're here now," she said again. "That's enough."

Annie had insisted on sleeping in his bed instead of her own, and he hadn't questioned the decision. Lucky didn't care which room they shared, as long as there was a bed in it.

Since he knew he couldn't stick around once the case was over, he should steer clear of her. At least he'd warned her that he couldn't stay. At least he wasn't the only one taking advantage of the situation; she'd told him plainly enough that he made the visions abate. Sometimes he even made them go away entirely. Maybe that's why she threw herself so wholeheartedly into making love. It was an escape, a respite from the visions that disturbed her.

Then again, maybe she just liked the sex. It was powerful enough to be enjoyable for its own sake.

She slept naked, and so did he. The hallway night-light burned softly, giving off just enough light to illuminate all but the deepest corners of the room. With Annie caught up against his side, he tried to sleep—and couldn't.

If her ability was real, and he was beginning to believe that was the truth, then how much did she know? Too much, that was certain, and that was just another reason for him to leave this place as soon as possible.

He was thirty-six years old, and he'd been married once. That relationship—the only serious relationship he'd ever had—had been an unmitigated disaster, enough so that he hadn't even considered committing himself to one woman since then. Did that make him a wuss? Or a very smart man? There had been a time when he'd had no doubt about the answer to that question, but right now—he wasn't so sure anymore.

If he ever did decide to settle down, maybe he should snag a woman like Annie. Sweet, funny, sexy, off-the-wall and full of surprises. He really should find someone without the psychic ability, though. It was a little creepy, knowing she might glimpse a thought or an image from his mind at any moment. How was a man supposed to get the upper hand when his woman knew what he was thinking?

His woman. It was an alarming idea, but he knew himself well enough to know that the minute Annie was out of danger she'd lose her appeal. At least, that was the way it usually worked. Still, he knew Annie was different from every other woman he'd ever known. She was special. She really and truly was his.

As if Annie instinctively knew he had awakened, she rolled to face him and opened her eyes. "You need your sleep," she said, her voice warm and sexy and more than a little dreamy. Her hand settled comfortably on his chest, and the fingers there rocked.

"If we're going to be involved, there are things you should know about me."

She sighed. "And you accuse me of being unfamiliar with the segue." Her eyes opened wider. "Wait a minute. Are we involved? I mean, more than—"

"Yes, dammit, we're involved."

Annie smiled and closed her eyes and made a sound rather like a satisfied cat. "And you said we have nothing in common...."

"I was married once."

That comment stole Annie's satisfied smile. Maybe she didn't know *everything* after all.

"It was a long time ago, and it didn't last more than a year. My wife left me when she found out about my father."

"It's stupid to blame a man for his father's actions, whatever they might be."

"You don't know?"

Again, her hand rocked against his skin, very naturally. "I don't know everything, Lucky, not even when we're this close. Thank goodness. I don't want to know everything. It would be paralyzing, I imagine." She settled against his chest, so that he could no longer see her face well. "You can tell me, if you'd like, but you don't have to. I like you. You're a good man. Nothing's going to change that."

He wanted to believe her, but a part of him didn't dare. Only a handful of people knew about his father. Once people knew the truth, they didn't look at him the same way anymore. His own wife had been afraid of him once she'd discovered the secret.

"My father was a hit man." This wasn't the time or the place for such a confession, but he found himself unable to keep the secret locked inside. Annie deserved to know. "Not even a very good one. He was cheap and sloppy, and he died in prison when I was twelve."

"Oh, Lucky," Annie murmured. She rose up just enough to look him in the eye. In the semidarkness they were nose to nose, chest to chest. "How awful for you."

"Don't feel sorry for me," he responded. "That's not why I told you. I just want you to understand why I can't stay here when this job is done, no matter what."

She cocked her head slightly. "What does your father have to do with us?"

Us. She said the word as if it meant something, and that couldn't happen. "Nothing at all," he answered, "unless you're appalled at the idea of sharing your bed with the offspring of a man who made his living killing people for money."

"I'm not, so now what?"

She was so guileless, so open and trusting and good,

he had no business sleeping with her. He didn't have to have her psychic powers to know that she wasn't the kind of woman who shared her body without sharing her heart, as well.

"I just thought you should know."

A soft smile spread across her face. "There's only one thing I want to know. What's your real name?"

"What?"

"Lucky must be short for something, or else you have a horrid given name that you don't want anyone to know. I could take a peek at your driver's license, but that doesn't seem fair."

"You'll peek into my head, but not my wallet?"

"A girl has to draw the line somewhere."

He'd just confessed the truth about his father to her, and moments later she made him smile. That had never happened before. "My name is Lucky."

"Your mother actually named you Lucky."

"Yes."

"I'm not sure that I believe you."

She grinned, and a conversation that had started out with a deadly seriousness turned to something comfortable and friendly. Annie made him smile at the oddest times and places. She reached past all the crap and touched him in a way no one else had in a very long time.

He could get used to this.

"Dreams tonight?" he asked, his hand finding her hair and one wayward blond strand.

"No, thank goodness."

"That's good." There was a thorough investigation

underway. With a little luck, the Benning Agency could find the killer without putting Annie through the torture of psychic nightmares. All they needed to do was identify more suspicious deaths and then tie them together through the people the victims had known. Eventually, their trail would come here, to Mercerville, and Annie's nightmares would end, once and for all.

"Stop it," she said softly. "Don't think about the case or the Huffs or work or nightmares."

"You're in my head again," he said, a soft accusation.

"I can't help it."

By the soft light that illuminated his bedroom, Annie was truly beautiful. Her gentle curves, her silky skin, her lively eyes. More, she had about and around her the most beautiful energy…and that was a thought he'd never had before.

"If you don't want me thinking about why I'm here, then you'd better distract me," he said. A kiss, an exploration of hands, reaching for another condom…

Annie's smile was positively wicked. "I think I can do that."

She surprised him by delving beneath the covers, bold and warm and fearless, and once there she distracted him very well.

Chapter 11

In spite of the terrifying events of the past few weeks, Annie felt indescribably wonderful, as if a warm glow had grown at the very center of her being, and all was truly right with the world. The glowy feeling was due to the sex in part, she knew that, but it was also much more than sex.

Lucky trusted her. He might never admit to that trust, but she knew it was there, as surely as she knew the sky was blue. She didn't have to peek into his head to know that. If he didn't trust her, he wouldn't have told her about his father. He wouldn't have given into late night pillow-talk that went well beyond the case that had brought him here and the physical need that had brought her into his bed. Even though she knew he wouldn't stay, the connection they had developed went far beyond anything she had ever known. In the end he would break her heart, but for a few days or weeks of this feeling…it was worth every moment of pain yet to come. She wouldn't miss this for all the world.

She still hadn't told Lucky about her vision of him in her bed, and she reasoned that as long as they remained in *his* bed, what they had couldn't be over. That was convoluted reasoning, perhaps, but it comforted her in some small way.

He didn't seem to mind where they slept, as long as it was together. This morning she'd awakened with his hands on her body, his mouth on the back of her neck, his honeyed whisper in her ear. Oh, my.

But there was more to Lucky's presence in her cabin and her life than sex, and they could not escape that fact in their waking hours. Today he was determined to eyeball a couple of the suspects they'd been able to come up with—which included any lone male who'd arrived in the area within the past year. Last night, he'd had a chance to observe Stu Bentley up close and personal, and even though Annie was positive her friend's husband couldn't be a murderer, Lucky refused to strike him from the list without more proof.

Psychic ability would be so much more convenient if it was foolproof, and if she could call up what she wanted to see. It didn't work that way, apparently. She could occasionally slip into the killer's mind, but she couldn't see him. Maybe if she'd honed her skills in the past, as her grandmother had urged her to do, she wouldn't be in this mess now.

According to what little Truman and Sadie had been able to learn about the suspects, Harrison Sharp, the new mailman, was the only one who'd been cleared. He'd moved here from Florida, and there was lots of paperwork—and even photos—to confirm his residence there. It shouldn't take long to clear or condemn the others, but it would take some time. A day or two or maybe three, Lucky had told her.

And then, when they discovered who'd killed the Huffs and the others, Lucky would be gone. That certainty dimmed her happiness, but she wouldn't let it ruin these last few days. She felt guilty to view the end of this case with even a hint of sorrow. The killer needed to be caught and put away, but oh, losing Lucky was going to be hard.

Her hand, which was caught securely in his, squeezed tightly as they entered the fudge shop. Wade Nance, who had bought the popular tourist stop a few months back, had kept on all the former employees and couldn't always be found in this shop. But he did spend a lot of time here. On slow days he could be seen going in and out, roaming the sidewalk and the nearby shops, trying to tempt passersby to try his sweets. When there were tourists in the area, the shop stayed busy.

Lucky studied the glass case. "I had no idea there were so many kinds of fudge," he said, his voice low, intended for her and her alone. One eye narrowed as he studied the chunks of candy on display.

"I like the lemon," Annie said.

Lucky shook his head. "Lemon fudge. That's just…wrong."

The girl behind the counter—pretty, longtime local Sara Clark—heard him, and immediately stepped forward with a sample of the lemon fudge. Lucky took it almost grudgingly, and after a moment's hesitation popped the small piece into his mouth. "Not bad," he admitted.

It looked as if Nance was out today, or else their suspect was in the back room. They couldn't see anyone but Sara in the shop. As she had with the others, Annie tried to imagine the man who owned the candy store—with the unoriginal name Fudge, Fudge, Fudge—as a murderer, and she couldn't do it. Of course, she couldn't imagine anyone doing what this serial killer had done. Only a monster was capable of such horrors, and in her mind there weren't such monsters in the world—certainly not in Mercerville.

Lucky said she was naive, and maybe he was right.

He ordered a quarter pound of the lemon fudge he proclaimed to be unnatural but tasty, and as Sara was weighing the candy, another couple wandered in. Gray-haired, plump and wearing matching T-shirts, they studied the display much as she and Lucky had. On their heels, another, younger couple came into the small shop. The girl squealed when she spotted the strawberry fudge.

A moment later, Wade Nance appeared. He must've heard the voices from the back room and realized that Sara needed help.

Annie couldn't say that she knew Nance well, but she had seen him around town and he'd come into the shop a couple of times when she'd been there. He never bought anything, but then he was a widower with no one to buy girlie things for. At least, that was what he told people. If he was the killer, that might not be the case.

Or maybe he'd killed his wife. A shudder crawled up her spine. Maybe he was a widower, but it was by choice. He didn't look at all threatening, but looks could be deceiving. While Lucky paid for the fudge, Annie moved in Nance's direction. He was on the other side of the counter, not even near being in reach. If she could touch him, even for a split second…

Nance sliced fudge for the older couple and wrapped it. As he worked he carried on conversation with the customers. He didn't discuss anything alarming or special. The weather. Football. Fudge, of course. The case was too high for Annie to reach across and touch him. She'd have to bound across the counter and tackle him, and wouldn't that be subtle. Not.

Wade Nance didn't look at all like a murderer. For one thing, he was too small to overpower two people. He didn't stand much taller than she, and he definitely didn't have Lucky's muscles. He was one of the most ordinary-looking men she'd ever known. His hair was a medium brown, his eyes the same. His clothes didn't fit exactly right, as if he'd bought the dark pants and golf shirt without trying them on, and then decided that to take them back and exchange them for the correct sizes would be too much trouble. Both articles of clothing needed to be ironed, and the pants needed to be hemmed an inch or so, but she supposed a widower wouldn't think of such things.

Most people had at least one striking or attractive feature, but not Nance. She tried to reach for him with her mind, without being obvious. She tried to turn on her psychic ability and bring on the sensations she usually tried to block. For a moment there was nothing, and then she heard a faint whisper in her mind.

The thoughts were as ordinary as the man. Rent. Salaries. Advertising. He'd obviously been working on the shop's books while in the back room. He was thinking about selling the shop, even though he hadn't been here all that long. There were no horrid, violent thoughts. No rage. She tried to reach deeper, but beneath the commonplace thoughts there was…nothing.

She shuddered. True emptiness was more terrifying than rage, and it was certainly sad. This little shop and the mundane details attached to it were all Wade Nance had in his life.

Lucky stood behind her, a small bag caught in one hand. His other hand settled comfortably and easily at the small of her back, but he didn't lead her from the store. He knew what she was thinking, what she planned to do, if she could find the chance.

When Nance's customers had paid and gone, Annie caught his attention with a wide smile. "Hello, Wade." The emptiness disturbed her. If she could touch him, just for a split second… "How about a sample of the maple fudge?"

He smiled at her. Not a wide smile, but more than a polite one. "You've never had the maple fudge?"

"Never."

"Now that's a real shame. We'll have to do something about that." He cut off a piece of the maple fudge, laid it on a small sheet of white bakery paper and handed it over the counter. Annie reached for the candy, holding her breath as her fingers brushed against Nance's.

Even though she touched him briefly, all she glimpsed were the same commonplace thoughts she'd caught from a distance. The day's receipts, the checks he had to write when the place was quiet again, whether or not he'd make a profit when he sold the shop. Beneath it all was a void left by his wife's departure, that emptiness she'd glimpsed even from a distance.

Nance's wife wasn't dead, though. She'd left him, years ago. He'd been telling people she was dead since she'd walked out.

"Give that a try. You might like it even better than the lemon."

Nance smiled as Annie popped a small piece of the sample into her mouth. "It's wonderful," she said after she swallowed the candy, "but I think the lemon is still my favorite."

She said goodbye. Hand in hand, she and Lucky left Fudge, Fudge, Fudge. She didn't breathe deeply until they were on the sidewalk.

"Well?" Lucky asked as they walked toward the garden shop, where—according to Annie's inquisitive phone calls that morning—carpenter Jim Ingram was supposed to pick up an order for Edith Kerr this afternoon.

"I didn't sense any violence or anger," Annie said, "just a very sad emptiness. He misses his wife very much."

"Could it be him?" Lucky asked sharply.

She squeezed his hand. "You want yes and no answers,

but sometimes that's not what I get. I don't know. I don't think so, but I can't say it's impossible, either."

"I'm not going to get that name and address, am I?" he teased.

"Maybe Truman and Sadie can come up with that kind of information. It's not exactly what I do."

Halfway between the fudge shop and the garden shop, Lucky stopped, spun her around and kissed her. It was a quick but very deep kiss, and oh, it was more than enough to make her think of the night to come.

Before he ended the kiss, a shiver walked up her spine. Someone was watching. No, *he* was watching.

Jim Ingram was not at all like the owner of the fudge shop. The carpenter, who hired himself out all over the county, was over six feet tall, and he was built like a moose. Drugs or no drugs, he could very easily overpower two ordinary people. His disposition wasn't exactly sunny.

Lucky was uneasy expecting Annie to get some sort of revealing reading from the big man, but it had to be done. She was the one who had set this into motion, after all, and for the ordeal to be over for her the man responsible for the Huffs' deaths had to be caught.

They entered the garden shop as Ingram was paying for his purchases—Edith Kerr's purchases, to be more specific. But Annie said the elderly woman wasn't getting around the way she used to, and Ingram had been doing more and more work for her lately. It had only taken two phone calls—disguised as inquiries into the handyman's workmanship and reliability—to find that out. Small towns were like that. Everyone knew everything. Well, almost everything.

The counter was piled high with garden flags and hand tools, and even a small statue.

"Gnomes are creepy. Have you ever noticed that?" Annie asked, her voice soft as they meandered down the wind chime aisle.

"There's goes my great idea for your Christmas present," he countered.

Annie laughed, and then with an almost startling suddenness the laughter stopped. Lucky knew why. He wasn't going to be anywhere near Mercerville at Christmastime.

"Anything?" he asked.

Her eyes turned toward Ingram, and she shuddered. "I don't like him," she whispered.

"Why not?"

"He's unhappy. His life is not what he wanted or expected it to be. He moves often, waiting for that happiness to find him, but…it never does."

"Is he our man?"

"I don't know." She turned her eyes to him. "I'm sorry. This would be so easy if I could see everything I want to see, but I can't. I see what I see."

"Will it help to touch him?"

He saw her gentle shudder and knew the idea of touching Ingram repelled her, but she didn't refuse. "It might."

They walked toward the front counter as the clerk was putting the garden flags and tools in a large paper bag. Ingram was obviously anxious to get out of the

store. One big foot tapped impatiently, and when the
salesgirl mentioned the nice weather, he just grunted.

She went to wrap the gnome in thick paper, so it
wouldn't get broken on the way home.

"It's so cute," Annie said as she reached past Ingram
and peeled back a bit of paper to look at the odious
creature. As she did so, her arm brushed against
Ingram's. The big man drew away from her as if she'd
hit him.

"There's plenty just like that one on aisle five,"
Ingram said sharply. Lucky didn't like the way the
handyman looked at Annie, his eyes narrowed and cold.

He took Annie's arm and pulled her gently away
from the counter. "Aisle five. Thanks."

They walked down aisle five, and without stopping
to look at the gnomes, they walked out of the garden
shop and into the sunlight of the crisp fall afternoon.

"Well?" he asked as they walked away from the store
and Jim Ingram.

"He's a very angry man," Annie said, and it seemed
that she moved closer. She shivered, and he put his arm
around her. "But I'm still not sure. Who else do we have
on our list?"

"Bill Stevens and Parker Glover, but they can wait
until tomorrow." Annie was exhausted by what little
they'd done so far. Maybe by tonight Sadie would have
more answers for him. More suspects cleared, or maybe
even more names added to the list.

For all they knew, the man they were looking for was
keeping such a low profile, no one in Mercerville even
knew he existed. He could be living well beyond this

town, driving in when he wanted to watch, living his life in another small town, or a big one where he could blend in. Worse, what if he'd been here all along, and the other suspicious deaths Truman had uncovered were unconnected? It was even possible that the man had been here for years, and had made a few long trips in the past four years. Maybe he had a vacation house nearby, as so many people from Nashville and Knoxville and beyond did. If any of those scenarios was the case, there was no telling when—or if—this case would be resolved.

Not that he was anxious to leave Mercerville and Annie behind, but he did want her to be out of danger. As long as she was having the dreams that pointed her toward the killer, she wasn't safe. She didn't want anyone to know of her ability because she didn't want her neighbors to know she was different. Lucky knew that if the killer realized she had reached into his head, she'd be next on his list.

As they approached Annie's Closet, the woman at his side came to an unexpected halt. She held her breath, and when she breathed again she muttered a vile word.

"What's wrong?" A vision, a prophesy, heartburn…anything was possible.

Annie pointed, and Lucky looked at the man who was leaning against the brick wall beside the front door to her shop. The man in question looked to be under thirty. His pale hair was cut too short, and he wore tight blue jeans and a gray T-shirt.

"Who's that?" It would be too much to ask for that she'd tell him that man who'd made her stop their progress was the murderer he was looking for.

"Um, that's Jerry."

"The sheriff's deputy you dated?" Somehow he'd expected a Barney Fife type, not a freakin' pretty boy.

"Yeah."

They resumed the trek, more slowly than before. "So, what's the problem? You said it wasn't serious."

Annie sighed. "I wasn't serious." She glanced over and up to catch Lucky's eye for a split second. "He was."

In outward appearance alone, Jerry Tinsdale was perfect. Physically, there wasn't a man in Mercerville who could hold a candle to the handsome deputy—or there hadn't been until Lucky had arrived.

Beyond the pretty, high-cheekboned face that could grace the cover of a romance novel or a Chippendales calendar, and killer blue eyes that could stop a woman in her tracks, there lurked…not much. Jerry wasn't overly smart, he wasn't witty. He certainly wasn't a great conversationalist. Their two dates had been sheer torture.

He had insisted all along that they looked great together. Annie was pretty sure that midway through the second date, he had their three blond-haired, blue-eyed children named.

"Hi, Annie," Jerry said. He had a smile for her, and then a glare for Lucky. How obvious could he be?

"Jerry, hi. What are you doing here?"

"It's, you know, my day off."

"I figured," she said. "No uniform."

Jerry rocked back on his boot heels. "I've been hearing about you and this guy, and I, you know, wanted to check him out." This statement was followed by another glare cast Lucky's way. In a flash, Annie knew that Jerry had practiced this glare in front of the mirror of his pristine bathroom, and she had to work very hard to withhold a laugh.

"Lucky Santana," Annie said with a wave of her hand, "this is Jerry Tinsdale."

"We dated," Jerry said as he reluctantly offered his hand to Lucky.

"I heard," Lucky responded.

Testosterone filled the air as they shook hands. With her senses on high alert, she could almost taste the testosterone. It was electric. Powerful. Since she'd never had two gorgeous men vying for her attention before, Annie savored the moment. She allowed herself to forget that Jerry was a male bimbo—a manbo, as it were—and that Lucky wouldn't be around any longer than it took to catch the killer. For now, at this moment, they both wanted her. She liked it. What woman wouldn't?

Her enjoyment didn't last long. Something unexpected stole her breath. A chill walked up her spine, and as an unexpected pain sliced through her back, she dropped.

Alerted to the problem by her gasp, Lucky caught her before she collapsed to the sidewalk. She tried to look around to see who hurt her, but no one was there. No one was even close to her but Lucky and a very bewildered Jerry. Still, she knew he was close. Too close. And somehow…somehow he realized she was a threat to him. Why else would that pain slice into her?

Jerry took a step back and said, "Uh, are you okay?"

"I think I sprained my ankle."

Jerry's expression was one of sheer confusion.

Manbo, indeed. "But you weren't even moving. How'd you do that?"

"Just one of those freak accidents, I guess."

"Oh."

Lucky put his arm around her, uttered a crisp and dismissive "See you later" to Jerry and guided her toward his car. At first Annie forgot to limp for Jerry's benefit, but halfway to the car she thought to add a gentle shift in her walk, for his benefit. Her back still hurt, but the pain was subsiding. Right now, she was more afraid than in pain.

When they were well away from Jerry, Lucky asked softly, "What the hell happened?"

Annie shuddered and leaned in as close to Lucky as was possible. "I think he's going to stab me in the back."

Chapter 12

Lucky's grip on the steering wheel was too tight as he turned into Annie's driveway. It had been that way since he'd pulled out of the parking spot on Main Street.

Annie had suffered a muscle spasm, and her imagination had run away with her. She was sensing the killer's attack on someone else. She was stressed-out, thanks to the situation, and that was to blame for her strange back spasm and vision. He was willing to believe anything but what Annie had told him.

His plan to turn the killer's eyes their way had seemed like a good one at the time. He wasn't naive, like the others had been. He would be on constant guard. There was no way the man who'd murdered the Huffs, and perhaps many others, could sneak up on Annie's cabin. He and Murphy had seen to that.

Besides, from what he'd learned, stabbing someone in the back wasn't this guy's style.

So Annie must be wrong.

Unless, of course, the killer learned what she could do, and he veered from his usual MO to take her out in the sneakiest and most cowardly way possible—with a knife in the back.

Since they'd turned onto the mountain road, Annie had been very quiet. It wasn't normal for her to be so silent and still. Normally she fidgeted; she chattered. She changed the subject without warning. Since he lived alone and often worked alone, Lucky liked silence. He enjoyed being alone. But right now he wanted to hear Annie chatter.

She waited until they were in the cabin, with the door locked behind them, before she looked at him and began to speak.

"My mother always hated the fact that I inherited some psychic ability from her mother. When I was little and I said something odd, she'd get this expression of horror on her face. No, it was more than horror. It was repulsion. No little girl wants her mother to look at her that way, and I can still remember that look as if she was standing here now."

Annie sat on the sofa, kicked off her shoes and tucked her feet beneath her. She quickly adopted a withdrawn pose.

Lucky sat beside her. He didn't know why she'd chosen this moment to tell him that her mother wasn't wild about her ability. Maybe she just wanted him to know, the way he'd wanted her to know about his father. "She was probably scared because she didn't understand."

"Who can understand?" Annie laid her head on his shoulder, but still she remained somehow distant, with her body drawn into itself. "In Nashville, when I went to the police with what I knew and ended up having to explain myself to the people in my life, I saw that same expression from my fiancé. He looked at me like I was a monster who was about to eat him up. I was the boogeyman jumping out of the closet, the guy with a chainsaw and a hockey mask. He hated me for not being the simple, ordinary girl he'd fallen in love with."

"That's all history," Lucky said. He wasn't accustomed to comforting people, but that was obviously what Annie needed. Comfort. A friend. Someone who understood what she was going through. He didn't exactly understand, but maybe he could comfort.

"I wish it was history," she said softly as she turned her head so she could look him in the eye. "You looked at me that way today, when I said he was going to stab me in the back. Did it just become real to you? Did it take that moment on the street for you to finally realize that I'm for real?"

He didn't want to hurt her, not this way. He didn't want to add his name to the long list of people who had disappointed her by not accepting who and what she was. "No. I accepted your ability days ago. I'm not revolted because you had a vision, not at all. I'm terrified at the idea of this guy getting close enough to you to hurt you."

"I know that," she whispered. "But still…you are a little freaked, and you might as well not try to hide it from me."

"Maybe a little freaked," he admitted.

"Maybe a little," she repeated, and then she laid her head on his shoulder again.

Did she understand that she had rocked his reality with her visions? Did she know that until he'd met her, he'd only believed in what he could hold in his hands? She did scare him, a little, but only because she touched him in a way no other woman ever had. He really hoped she couldn't see that, because getting too close to Annie was a weakness he couldn't afford.

Annie buried her face against Lucky's chest, taking in his strength, his solidness, his warmth. If he knew how well she could see into him now, he wouldn't be here. He'd run away, send another agent to watch over her, never look back. She wasn't ready for him to go.

Even though the pain was gone—and in truth, it hadn't lasted more than a split second—Annie could still feel the sharp agony of the knife slicing into her flesh. More, she felt the very real fear of knowing a killer was right behind her, and that she was alone with no one to help her.

Right now she *wasn't* alone, so she closed her eyes and let the fear go.

"What if we're wrong?" she asked.

"Wrong about what?" Lucky brushed his fingers through her hair, in an absent fashion.

"Everything. The killer, the suspects, the other crimes Sheriff McCain found, the people he's watching…everything."

"Between your dreams and the factual evidence, we should be on track."

Her heart hitched. "What if the dreams are wrong? I haven't honed this skill. Instead I've done my best to shut it down. I've fought it and denied it and dismissed it. If I'd listened to Grams instead of my mother, if I'd practiced and grown stronger instead of purposely weakening my gift, then I could be sure. Right now I'm not sure of anything."

She wasn't sure of anything at all, except the crazy and inescapable notion that she was falling in love with Lucky Santana. Was he another gift she would willingly throw away? If she told him how she felt, would he immediately draw away from her, physically and emotionally? As well as she could see into his mind, she still wasn't sure.

So she kissed him. Physically, there were no doubts in her mind, or his. She couldn't get enough of Lucky, and he was mystified by the strength of his need for her. For now, that was enough.

They kissed and touched for a while, gratefully forgetting the sad events that had brought him here, her violent visions, his promise that this relationship was temporary. Then they began to undress one another—without haste or even a touch of urgency. They had all afternoon and all night, and nothing else mattered, for a while.

When she uncovered the scar on his shoulder, she kissed it. She kissed it, and then she traced the scar with the tip of her tongue. She wanted to draw out the pain of this old scar, take it into herself for him. There was no actual physical pain for Lucky, but to be stabbed by the woman he loved, his own *wife*…how horrible for him. It was much more horrible than the fear-filled glances of loved ones that still haunted her.

Lucky bared her breasts and teased the nipples much as she had teased his scar. Annie gratefully and completely forgot everything but his touch and the warm promise of what was to come—pleasure, a soul-deep bond, peace.

Love?

More undressed than not, they could've kept going without pause and made love on the couch—but of course that couldn't happen. The condoms Lucky had bought were in the spare bedroom, and a man who didn't plan to stick around once the job was done didn't take chances where the possibility of procreation was concerned.

It would be nice if she could tell Lucky that she wouldn't get pregnant, but she didn't see that clearly into herself. Some segments of her future were crystal clear, but most were foggy—or dark.

"Your room or mine?" Lucky asked as he rose from the couch and took Annie's hand to assist her to her feet.

She fell gently against him so her bare chest rested against his. "Yours."

As long as that image of Lucky in her bed persisted, she knew the opportunity hadn't passed. She wasn't ready for this relationship, temporary as it might be, to be over.

Lucky lifted her off the floor, and she wrapped her legs around his hips as he carried her to his bed. Annie buried her face against his neck and kissed, and she allowed everything else to fade away. Like a fog on the mountain burned away by the sun, all her fears and uncertainties faded away.

He laid her on the bed, finished undressing himself and her, and then he lowered his body to rest on hers. Lucky never rushed, no matter how ready he was to be inside her. He never entered her until she was on the edge of hurtling out of control, and then...

This afternoon was no different. He aroused her until her breath wouldn't come and her body trembled with need, and then he pushed inside her. He made love to her, slow at first and then fast. Everything went away while he loved her. Every worry, every fear, every bad memory. There was nothing but her body and his, perfectly linked and reaching for fulfillment.

They came together, clutching one another with a combination of ferocity and tenderness. And in the trembling haze that followed Annie had one moment of clarity.

She loved him.

They knew. He didn't know how, but...they *knew*.

It was well dark once again, but instead of watching the Bentleys' house tonight, he watched Annie Lockhart's cabin. He remained at a distance, with his binoculars trained on the warmly lit windows. He couldn't see anything beyond those windows, since the curtains were closed.

Word had gotten around quickly enough that Lucky Santana was looking into the Huffs' deaths, but most people didn't give that news much credence. After all, officially it was a cut-and-dried murder/suicide, and no one questioned those findings. Well, the victims' families had had lots of questions in the beginning, but even they had grown quiet lately. He assumed that someone from the Huff family had hired Santana to investigate the incident, but he wasn't certain.

Why was Annie with Santana, as he poked his nose where it did not belong? Yes, they were romantically involved, but why on earth would she accompany him as he questioned people around town? Maybe she was serving as a sort of cover. Did Annie even know what her lover was up to, or was she an innocent pawn in his inconvenient investigation? Somehow, he thought she did know.

They both knew too much.

They hadn't uncovered his identity, but if they kept asking questions and digging where they should not, would they? In four years, no one had unraveled one of his carefully constructed scenes. How could they? He made sure there were no red flags at the scenes of his victims' deaths, nothing suspicious to raise unwanted questions. And since all the killings took place in rural communities where there were minimal facilities for investigation, no one looked beyond the obvious.

If Annie and Santana continued to ask questions, they might find something he'd missed. He couldn't think of anything that might point the investigation toward murder by someone other than Trey Huff, but it was possible. Worse, what if they got others asking questions? What if other investigators in other states began to look more closely at suspicious cases from the past? Then where would he be?

His grip on the binoculars tightened. He could move on to another town and forget about the Bentleys, but if he vanished now, would their investigation turn to him? If that happened they'd surely go back and find evidence of other crimes. He couldn't afford to display suspicious behavior. Not now.

He also couldn't allow those two to keep poking their noses where they didn't belong, but what was he supposed to do? Panic was never the answer. He had to remain calm in the face of this new challenge. Maybe they were looking…but they had nothing. Nothing at all.

Still, Annie and Santana did bear watching, and if by some miracle they got too close, he'd know. He'd know.

"You know about the scar, don't you?" Lucky felt Annie's body, which was bare and resting against his as if it had been made to fit there, stiffen.

"Would you feel better if I lied to you and said no?"

He knew Annie wouldn't lie to him. It wasn't her style. "Not really."

She rose up slightly, propping herself on his chest so she could look him in the eye. The only light came from the hallway, but it was enough. It was enough to make his heart do strange things when he looked into Annie's eyes.

"She was scared."

"Of me."

"I didn't say she had reason to be scared, just that she was. Her fear was irrational, but to her it was real." Annie cocked her head.

When his wife had found out about his father, she'd freaked. She'd accused him of lying about who he was, of hiding his past. Of course he'd hidden facts about his past. Who wants to brag to the woman he plans to spend his life with that his father was a hired killer? He'd convinced himself that it wasn't important, but Cherie had thought differently. She'd always been emotionally fragile, unable to handle even the smallest upset. Still, Lucky had been so sure she could handle this crisis. He'd been wrong. When he'd tried to convince her that there was no reason to turn on him because of something his father had done, she'd panicked and defended herself with a kitchen knife.

He'd been so surprised when the knife had pierced skin.

Looking back, he understood more clearly what had happened. Cherie's home life before their marriage had been less than wonderful. It was no wonder that she was fragile. Perhaps even a little unstable. Her father had been an abusive drunk, and marrying a man she'd thought to be a complete straight arrow had been her escape. Finding out he was not precisely who he'd claimed to be had torn her neat world apart.

He'd tried to save Cherie from a sad and unsafe home life, and his thanks had been a twisting knife in the shoulder and a shrill scream for him to get away from her. The pain of the knife hadn't been the worst of it. He'd loved her, and she hadn't been able to get past the truth of his heritage—or the fact that he'd lied to her about it.

Lucky felt a twisting in his gut. He'd loved his wife, but looking back…what he'd felt for her hadn't been any stronger or more real than what he felt for Annie. In truth, it had been a pale version of what he felt for the woman in his arms. That was scary.

His track record sucked.

"I can't say I'm sorry," Annie said softly. "If you were still with her, you wouldn't work for the

Benning Agency, and you certainly wouldn't be here. You also wouldn't be happy. Sometimes you think if that…that incident hadn't happened you'd still be married, and you'd have two or three kids and a dog, and you'd be happy, but that's not true. She was wrong for you, and if you were still together, you'd both be miserable."

"Gee, thanks."

She smiled. "Everything that has happened to us has brought us to this point, so right now I can't even complain about what happened to me in Nashville, or how Seth and my mother were horrified by what I can do. I can't wish my abilities or my nightmares away, because they brought you to me."

He didn't want Annie to make more of this relationship than she should, because wanting more than they could have would only make the end more difficult. No matter how he felt about her, it would have to end— eventually.

"I know, I know." She laid her head down once again. "Don't remind me."

"I didn't say a word."

"You didn't have to."

He should be terrified that this woman could actually read his mind, but he wasn't. It had been a long time since he'd allowed anyone to get this close, and he wasn't sure it was wise—even now.

He'd tried so hard to save Cherie, and he'd failed. Since then he'd been trying to save every damsel in distress that crossed his path. Sometimes he succeeded, but some people simply didn't want to be saved.

At least he had learned not to make promises beyond the moment.

"So, you dated that Jerry guy twice?"

Once again, Annie lifted her head. She smiled widely. "You're changing the subject."

"Yes, I am. *Twice?*"

Annie sighed. "It was a totally female faux pas, I'm sad to confess. He's so good-looking, I was hoping that on the first date he was just having a bad day. No one that handsome could really be that...dull."

"Say it, Annie. The guy's dumb as a rock."

"Yeah, he's a manbo."

"Manbo?"

"Male bimbo, and don't be so critical. You've dated women just like him, many of them more than *twice*."

It was true enough, so he let the subject drop. Annie laid her head down again. In the dark, her breathing grew deep and even. One of her fine legs slipped between his and rested there, fitting nicely. For a long while she didn't move at all, but to breathe. He thought she was asleep when she whispered, "I don't want to dream tonight."

He didn't want her to. She'd done enough. In fact, she'd done too much. Annie shouldn't be in danger because she had this inherited gift that had crashed down on her well-ordered life.

"If you don't sleep, you can't dream."

"True enough."

Lucky rolled Annie onto her back, drew down the covers and kissed the soft, sweet flesh between her breasts. She closed her eyes and sighed, sexy and content. When he aroused her, her psychic ability faded dramatically. She'd told him that much, more than once. Maybe now was a safe time to wonder why it was that he felt so close to this woman. It was more than his usual protective instinct. More than a job. More than sex. And dammit, he couldn't allow that to happen. He spread Annie's thighs gently, and stroked. She opened for him…only for him.

He kissed her soft belly and whispered against pale, silky skin, "Don't worry about dreams tonight. We have better things to do than sleep."

Chapter 13

Annie got her wish. She eventually slept, but she didn't dream. At least, not that she remembered. She didn't know if it was Lucky, exhaustion, or sheer stubbornness that won out over the psychic nightmares, but her sleep was peaceful.

Not just for one night, but for two...and then three.

During their waking hours, Lucky watched her like a hawk. He was vigilant, and that was stating it mildly. He didn't question anyone when they went to town, and the displays of affection meant to draw in the killer were relegated to private moments when no one else could see. He declared their active investigation over and done, saying someone else could investigate their suspects, from a distance.

They shopped when necessary, they ate in a couple

of the local restaurants and Annie spent some time in her two stores, which was also necessary. Lucky continued to receive information from the other employees of his agency—those to whom he had handed the investigation. Sadie and Murphy were the most involved. They managed to eliminate some of the suspects and rule out some of the suspicious deaths they had suspected might be connected to the Huffs'. Some accidents and random crimes were just that.

Sadie had told her old partner that it could take weeks—maybe even months—to investigate all the suspicious deaths they found. There was no guarantee that they could find a connection, even if they discovered similar murders. For all they knew, the killer had changed his name, his appearance…everything. This news put Lucky in a bad mood like Annie had never seen. He was worried about her, and in a way that made her wish she hadn't told him about the vision of being stabbed.

But oh, she would hate to face that prediction alone.

Lucky paced in her great room. Now and then he stopped pacing to feed the fire, which warmed the cabin on this cold, autumn night. Winter was coming. She tried to imagine Lucky here when the first snow came, but she couldn't. She couldn't be angry about that, since he'd never promised her that he'd be here for longer than it took to solve this crime.

"Maybe he's moved on," Lucky suggested as he paced. "We spooked him, and he left the area. That's why you haven't had any more dreams. The physical proximity you need for the visions to materialize just isn't there anymore."

"In a way I wish you were right, but if that's the case, then we failed. If he's run, then he got away."

Lucky snapped his head around and glared at her. "As long as he's nowhere near you, I don't really care. Let someone else catch him. Neither of us is responsible for every bad guy in the world."

His anger touched her, because she understood the protective nature of that rage. Maybe Lucky was following his usual pattern of love 'em and leave 'em, but whether he'd admit it or not, he did care for her in a deeper way than he'd ever intended.

"No," she said, "but like it or not, I think we're responsible for this one."

A subtle, disbelieving lift of Lucky's eyebrows conveyed to her his feelings on that subject—as if she needed such a blatant hint to tell her what he was thinking.

He had begun this case determined to prove her wrong in all ways. He'd intended to prove that she wasn't psychic and the Huffs had died just as the sheriff said they'd died, in a tragic murder/suicide in which no third party was involved. When he'd finally realized that she and her dreams were for real, his intent had turned to catching a killer.

Now, tonight, his sole objective was to protect her. There was little else on his mind.

"I'm not going to leave," she said as she watched him wear a path in her throw rug.

Lucky stopped pacing and glared at her. "The least you could do is wait for me to suggest *out loud* that you move away until we catch the guy."

She gave him a soft smile. "Sorry."

"Moving away until the killer is caught is the best solution."

"I have a business to run."

"You also have two very capable managers. The business will survive."

"This is my home. Why should I let some psycho make me run away?"

"Maybe because he could kill you?" Lucky snapped. "Maybe because you felt him drive a knife into your back? I know you're glad the dreams and visions have stopped, but what if he's found a way to block you? What if he now has the ability to sneak up on you, because you can't see what he's thinking anymore?"

"He always had the ability to sneak up on me. I've never seen everything, Lucky, especially not where my life is concerned. Almost all of my visions pertaining to the unknown relate to other people, not myself."

"Almost," he said, throwing the word back at her.

How had this man become such an important part of her life in such a short time? Love was supposed to take time. It was supposed to grow slowly, spreading deep roots that would not be easily shaken. A couple was supposed to take the time to get to know one another well before they felt this…love.

Of course, she couldn't possibly know Lucky any better than she did right now. She'd glimpsed the very heart of the man, and that glimpse only made her love him more.

Lucky was still afraid of love, so it would be best to keep her romantic feelings to herself.

"You never did tell me what Lucky is short for?"

"Yes, I did. It's not short for anything. My name is Lucky. Lucky Rawlins Santana."

"Rawlins?"

"My mother's maiden name." He'd mentioned his mother a couple of times, and on both occasions she'd felt him shut down inside. He didn't want her to see this part of his past, and she had done her best not to pry. Whatever had happened to his mother…it was dark, and Lucky carried that pain with him as surely as he carried the pain of his scar.

Annie tried a dismissive smile. She didn't want to push or pry. "No wonder you don't go by your middle name."

He cocked his head and started at her. "You don't see it, do you?"

"It's private. I'm trying not to see."

"I appreciate that," he said in a lowered voice.

"I can see that it hurts," she said, wanting to be honest with him…always. Except where the love thing was concerned, of course.

Lucky quit pacing. He sat beside her and draped his arm over her shoulder. It was a casual pose, but there was nothing casual about this man or their relationship. "Diane Rawlins came from a very prestigious and wealthy family. They lived in the best house in a small town in Mississippi, and her daddy owned most of the local businesses, as well as most of the town. She had three brothers, but Diane was the only Rawlins daughter, and she was the princess of the town. It was assumed that she'd marry the boy she dated in high school. They were perfectly suited. His family didn't have as much money, but they were one of *the* families.

You know, tracing ancestors back to the Civil War, throwing teas for all the right people, deciding who would and would not be accepted." His voice took on a decided edge of bitterness.

"But Diane had other ideas. She met Luis Santana, fell in love with him and eloped. By the time she found out that Luis had married her for her money, she was pregnant with me. The family made it clear that Luis Santana wasn't getting a dime of the family fortune, which did not go over well with my papa." His entire body stiffened. "He kicked my mother out of his house and told her to go home." Lucky stared at the fire...not at Annie.

Annie felt the anger and hurt in Lucky grow. No, it didn't grow. It was too old to grow. What it did was seep out of the corners of his soul, a pain he usually kept well hidden. She wanted to tell him to stop, to put the pain back where it belonged, to hide it well once again. But she didn't. She let him talk, uninterrupted.

"She tried to go home but they wouldn't let her. She worked minimum wage jobs, taking anything she could get in order to put food on the table. No one would give her half a chance to make amends, to...start over. Maybe if she hadn't been pregnant with me things would've been different, but she was, and people couldn't, or wouldn't, forget.

"Eventually she left this small town and moved to New Orleans. I was born. My father went to prison a few months later."

Annie knew this was a story Lucky didn't tell often, and still...it was a very real part of him. It wasn't fair that something he'd had no part in, something that had happened before he'd been born, had affected his life in this way. She let her fingers stroke his arm, very gently. Lucky spent his life taking care of people. Did he ever let anyone take care of him?

"I have some memories of my mother," he said. "She did her best, and I can still remember how she laughed sometimes. She was pretty, very pretty, and after a while in New Orleans…she ended up working as an exotic dancer." He glanced at Annie quickly. "She was a stripper. When I was nine, my mother got involved with one of the men who frequented the club where she worked. A few months later, he killed her."

"Oh, Lucky. I'm so sorry." Annie didn't see what had happened to Diane Santana, but she did feel a small boy's confusion and anger and heartbreak when his mother didn't come home.

"They sent me home to live with my grandparents, who were none too happy to have a mixed breed son of a hired killer and a stripper in their fine home. They made up a story about where my mother had been, so as not to damage their own reputations. As for my father, well, they just didn't mention him at all.

"But people knew, and they never let me forget. I tried so hard to be the perfect kid, and it got me beat up, laughed at and eventually stabbed by the woman I married right after I turned nineteen. Cherie's family lived out in the country. They weren't exactly connected to the people in town who knew everything, in spite of the tale my grandparents tried to spin." He had never considered, until this moment, that maybe that was why he'd been drawn to her in the first place. That and her obvious need to be rescued. "She didn't know about my father when we eloped, but enough people did know the truth and it wasn't long before someone made the effort to tell her exactly who she'd married. I guess when we eloped I should've just kept on running. But I didn't." He took a deep breath and exhaled slowly. "There you have it, the story of my life."

Annie laid a hand on Lucky's whisker-rough cheek and made him look at her. "That's not the story of your life," she said softly. "The story of your life began after you left that town. It began when you became a soldier, when you became a cop, when you went to work for the major, when you dedicated yourself to helping people. Your life began when you…"

When you walked into this cabin. She couldn't very well say that without telling Lucky that she loved him, and he wasn't ready to hear it.

"Your life begins anew every day."

"That's New Age crap," he said brusquely.

"It's the truth, but only if you let it be."

His answer was a kiss. Not a sweet one, but a deep kiss that stole her breath and very neatly changed the subject. They kissed, and held one another close, and soon he placed his hand between their bodies and slipped it between her legs, where he rubbed gently…but not too gently.

When Annie had a chance to take a deep breath, she said, "Sex isn't the answer to everything."

His response was a husky "Why not?"

* * *

What had he been thinking? He didn't tell anyone about his parents or his awkward growing up years in hickville Mississippi. Somehow Annie had gotten under his skin, and that was bad. Very bad. The only way to handle the knowledge that he was getting too close was to back off.

Lucky had never been known for his subtlety, and this situation was no different. When she left his bed on Sunday morning, Annie knew that whatever they'd had was over. He could tell the moment he saw the expression on her face, as she walked into the kitchen where he was making coffee, that anything of their relationship that went beyond business was finished.

It was one of the benefits of sleeping with a psychic. He was able to bypass the awkward explanations that came with the end.

If she was a really good psychic she'd known all along this wouldn't last, so she shouldn't even be surprised. She looked a little surprised, though, and even a little hurt.

It would be almost funny if things weren't so awkward. When he'd come here he hadn't believed it was possible that she—or anyone else—had psychic abilities. Now he was relying on those abilities to save him from painful explanations.

The fact that their relationship was over didn't mean he was going to lie down on the job. He was just as determined to find the man who'd invaded her dreams and lock him up so he could never hurt Annie—or anyone else, for that matter. Right now Annie was his responsibility, so keeping her safe was the number one priority.

Annie poured a cup of coffee and sat at the kitchen table. She crossed her legs, which were bare and very fine, beneath the long, oversized Drama Queen T-shirt. Lucky waited for an argument, but no argument came. He was supposed to be relieved that Annie knew without a messy scene that the relationship was over, but instead he felt as if things were incomplete. It had never been about anything but sex, anyway, so maybe she was as relieved as he was.

If she pressed for explanations or excuses, he could always argue that she insisted that he made her visions abate, and they needed every advantage they could get at the moment. If he made the visions stop, then he had no choice but to back off.

When Annie finished her coffee she set the cup in the sink and headed for the door. She had a morning ritual. Coffee. Shower. Some off-the-wall outfit with lots of color and maybe some bling, and then to work—either here or at one of her stores. Since it was Sunday, she wouldn't be going to either of the stores, but she wouldn't waste the day. Within the hour she'd be working on a design or a detailed froufrou purse.

As she left the room she glanced over her shoulder. Those blue eyes were strong and calm, tearless but a little sad. "You're wrong," she said. "We had a lot more than sex going for us."

Annie shampooed her hair vigorously. Dammit. She'd known all along that Lucky wasn't permanent, so it shouldn't hurt this much. The moment she'd opened her eyes this morning, leaving behind perfectly lovely dreams, she'd known that he'd pulled away from her, and that as far as he was concerned their little fling was over.

Tough as Lucky was, he was afraid of getting too close to anyone. He had huge trust issues, which was understandable given what his wife had done to him. He'd believed that he'd found a woman who would stand by him through thick and thin, and then she'd panicked and attacked him. He probably didn't want to hear that his wife hadn't been the sharpest knife in the drawer, and when she'd learned the truth she'd only been able to see the pain of her own childhood, not the brightness of her future away from that childhood. They'd both been so young... How could he allow anything that had happened then to stay with him?

Maybe because it wasn't the only rejection in his life. His father had rejected him before he was born, then his mother went and died on him. His grandparents, who had taken over parental duties after their daughter's death, had twisted everything and blamed a child for all that had gone wrong in their carefully laid plans for their child. What he didn't know was that the only way they could absolve themselves of their responsibility in their daughter's death was to place the blame elsewhere...on an innocent child who'd needed their love and never received it.

In a way, Annie hated Sadie McCain. Lucky might not love her, but he did trust her, and that was momentous, for him. Like it or not—love or not—Annie had put herself into the well-populated category of expendable women whose only purpose was to warm Lucky's bed.

When he'd told her so much about his mother and his childhood, she should've known he'd panic and step back. He likely wouldn't agree that's what he'd done, but she knew.

She understood Lucky better than he understood himself.

At the moment, Lucky considered their relationship, such as it was, done and over. But he still hadn't come to her bed, and no matter what he had decided, she didn't think of them as finished. Maybe it was wishful thinking on her part. Were her hopes for more getting in the way of what she knew to be true? It wasn't as if her psychic abilities were flawless.

She closed her eyes and rinsed the shampoo from her hair. Standing in the warm fall of water, she tried to let her heartbreak wash away. Her life had been good before Lucky came into it; it would be good again, one day.

But until then…

Pain sliced deeply into her back, in the exact same spot she'd felt that agony while standing on the Mercerville sidewalk days ago. She gasped, her knees buckled and she fell to her knees on the slick shower floor. The pain radiated from the point in her back all through her body. Her neck, her arms, her legs… The pain spread until she felt it everywhere. A dark fall of hair fell past her face, all but blinding her, and a trickle of blood swirled with the water from the shower, growing deeper and redder with every passing second. She smelled…she smelled something familiar that she couldn't identify. How could she identify the smell when she was in such pain?

The bathroom door swung open, and Lucky was there. He turned off the shower and reached for her, helping her to her feet and out of the shower, grabbing the fat white towel she'd placed nearby and wrapping her in it.

Annie let herself lean into him. He held her, and would not allow her to fall. "How did you know I was in trouble?"

He snorted. "The scream was a dead giveaway."

"I didn't scream."

"Yes, you did. What happened?"

Her panic began to fade, and she remembered. She had screamed, hadn't she? And that fall of dark hair, and the smell…

"It's not me," she whispered. "The stabbing, the knife…it's Kristie. Oh my God, the killer's been watching Kristie and Stu."

Lucky made her look at him. "Has the stabbing already happened or is it going to happen?"

"I don't know."

He led her from the bathroom and made her sit on her bed. Her bed. Overhead, the fan whirred gently. She trembled to the bone. Lucky grabbed her bedside phone, asked for the number of the bed-and-breakfast and dialed. When Kristie answered the phone, he ordered her to come to Annie's cabin. Now.

Annie could tell that Kristie tried to argue, but of course Lucky wouldn't have any of that. Very soon, Kristie agreed to obey his command. Annie suspected curiosity was the reason more than anything else.

Lucky hung up the phone and turned to stare at Annie with cold, strong amber eyes. "She's on her way."

"What about Stu?"

"Can you assure me that Stu wasn't the one doing the stabbing?"

"No, but…"

"That's why." He headed from the room with purpose in his step. "Get dressed. You've got some explaining to do."

She wanted to argue, but didn't. If it meant saving Kristie's life, then what choice did she have?

For a long moment after Lucky closed the door behind him, Annie remained on the bed, motionless. For the first time, tears stung her eyes. She was going to lose everything all over again. The guy, her friends…her home.

Love.

Chapter 14

"You're a...what?" Kristie perched on the edge of Annie's couch, and cocked her head to one side like a confused puppy.

"Psychic," Annie said in a flat, emotionless voice. "I have prophetic dreams, I sometimes know what people are thinking and every now and then I can catch a glimpse of the future. Psychic," she said again.

After a stunned moment of complete silence, Kristie grinned widely. "Okay, I get it. This is a joke, right?" She glanced at Lucky, looking for confirmation.

Lucky shook his head crisply, and there must've been something about his expression that convinced her that this was no joke. The grin disappeared and a new light came into the young woman's eyes. Fear.

There was more, and it had to be said, like it or not.

When Annie faltered, Lucky jumped in and told the story—in as few words as possible and without getting into anything too personal. He told Annie's friend about her dreams, the Huffs' deaths looking suspicious, their attempt to draw out the killer and finally, Annie's visions of being stabbed and her belief that Kristie was the intended victim.

Kristie jumped up off the couch. "I have to call Stu. Did you call him on his cell when you called me? He went to town to pick up some—"

Lucky laid a hand on the woman's shoulder. "Sit down. We haven't called Stu, and until he's eliminated as a suspect, we can't."

Until that moment Kristie had been stunned, confused and even frightened. The mention of her husband's name as a murder suspect brought anger to the surface.

"Stu wouldn't hurt a fly!" She had to look up to stare into Lucky's eyes, but she did just that. She didn't flinch or back down an inch. "How dare you? Just because we haven't been in town that long, you think you can accuse him of murder? What kind of investigation is this?" Her anger grew. "Psychic my…my butt. Annie, you've let this guy snow you, I can tell. You had some bad dreams and he convinced you that they're more than dreams for some reason I don't understand. How could you possibly think…?"

"Calm down," Annie said gently. "Getting all riled up isn't good for the baby."

Kristie turned to face Annie, who remained seated on the sofa, and her face paled considerably. "How do you know about the baby? We haven't told anyone, I haven't even seen a doctor yet. I sent Stu to the next county over to get the pregnancy test so there wouldn't be any gossip! So, how do you *know?*"

Annie remained calm. Too calm. "I told you how I know." She remained very still, waiting for her worst fear to come true. She waited for her friend to turn on her, to reject her, to be appalled by what she could do.

Kristie walked away from Lucky, all of her attention focused on the woman seated on the couch. Lucky wanted to yank her back, to make sure that she didn't have a chance to hurt Annie with her anger and her fear.

The dark-haired girl sat beside Annie, and after a moment she slipped her arm around Annie's stiff shoulder. "Oh, honey," she said tenderly, dismissing her own problems for a moment. She placed her head on Annie's shoulder. "What a mess. Well, hell, what are we going to do now?"

Lucky left the women alone, stepping onto the porch and flipping his cell phone open. He found Sadie on speed dial and made the call.

"Hi," Sadie said as she answered, knowing from the caller ID that he was on the line. "What's up?"

"Stu Bentley," Lucky said without preamble. "Drop everything and concentrate on him."

"Do you think he's the one?" A trace of crisp excitement entered her voice.

"No," Lucky said, "I don't. I want him cleared ASAP."

"I'll do my best," she said, the excitement gone as quickly as it had appeared. Sadie might be a wife and mother these days, but Lucky knew there were times when she missed her old job. This was apparently one of those times.

Lucky slipped his phone into his pocket, but he didn't go back into the cabin. He heard muffled tears from beyond the front door. He hated tears.

For a few long moments he leaned against the post by the front steps, looking at nothing, doing his best to feel nothing. He barely knew Kristie Bentley. He didn't even like her much.

But man, he didn't want her child to grow up with a murderer for a father. He didn't want the people of Mercerville to look at the kid years from now and whisper about the time Stu Bentley had committed murder. He didn't want them to talk about how the apple didn't fall far from the tree, and he didn't want them to talk about how "blood will tell."

As if this job hadn't been personal enough already…

Annie waited for Kristie to realize what was happening and draw away in horror, but for now the two women cried and hugged and cried some more. Annie didn't cry easily, but Kristie's tears were contagious. Kristie, whose life was in danger, whose husband had just been named as a murder suspect, had reason to cry.

As for Annie…it took her a moment to realize that the tears were for everything she was about to lose. Lucky, most of all. Maybe this was her curse. Maybe she was destined to lose every man she ever loved. Why could she only have love for a short while? Why couldn't it last?

Eventually the tears dried. Kristie sniffled and drew away, and Annie waited for the questions and the accusations to start.

Instead of tossing out accusations, Kristie sighed and placed a comforting hand on Annie's arm. "Oh, honey. This must be so difficult for you."

Obviously she didn't yet understand. "Lucky's not conning me. Everything I've told you is true."

"I know," Kristie said reluctantly. "As soon as you told me about the baby, I knew it wasn't a joke or a scam." She cocked her head to one side. "You really can see things, huh?"

"Sometimes. The ability has been quiet for a while, but the dreams about the Huffs' murders brought it back. It comes and goes, and I have no control, but to be honest, it's stronger than it's ever been."

"Are you getting any rest at all, with these terrible dreams disturbing your sleep?"

Annie started slightly. She had been prepared for a strong reaction, but not concern for her well-being. "Some. You're not…scared of me?"

Kristie gave Annie a wan smile. "Of course not. Why should I be scared of you?"

"Some people are, when they find out what I can do."

Again Kristie sighed. "*Some people* are idiots." She leaned against the back of the sofa and laid one hand over her still-flat belly. "When I found out I was pregnant, I smelled my mother's favorite perfume. Just for a second, but I definitely smelled it."

Annie knew that Kristie's mother had been dead three years.

The mention of phantom smells reminded Annie that she'd smelled something during her painful vision in the shower. She couldn't remember what, exactly, since she'd been entirely focused on the pain. But there had been a familiar odor…

"I smelled that perfume during the wedding ceremony, when Stu and I got married, and there are times when I just feel like she's there. Even if I don't smell or see anything, I just know she's standing with me. I've never told anyone about that, because I figure they'll think I'm nuts." She managed a smile. "I know what's happening to you isn't the same thing, but the world is filled with things we don't understand. All I know is that my mother visits me, and she comes from a good place. What's happening to you, it comes from a good place, too. There's no reason for me, or anyone else, to be afraid of you."

Annie relaxed. She felt it in her entire body, as if tension in her muscles and her skin and her very blood released. "Thank you," she said softly, her voice almost breaking. Lucky and Kristie both accepted what she could do. Lucky had a logical explanation for how her brain worked, and Kristie believed the ability came from "a good place." Whatever their rationale might be, they didn't hate her. They weren't afraid of her.

"No reason to thank me," Kristie said, her voice turning slightly more pragmatic. "We have work to do apparently."

"We?"

"Stu is not a killer. How can we prove it? Can you do your thing and see that he's innocent?"

"I haven't been able to do that so far. I'm seeing into the killer's brain, I've tapped into his thoughts a few times, but I don't see anything around him."

"What if you, like, touched some of Stu's things at the house. Would that help?"

"Maybe."

"Well, then, let's go."

Annie reached out a stilling hand as Kristie started to rise. "Wait. You stay here. I'll get Lucky to take me to the house."

"No way. I'm going with you."

Too many people had already been hurt. Annie didn't want Kristie, who knew her secret and didn't despise her, to be next. "I know you think Stu is innocent, but are you willing to risk your life, and the life of your baby, in order to prove it?"

"I don't *think* Stu is innocent," Kristie said calmly. "I know it. He would never hurt me, or anyone else."

Annie wanted to believe that was true, but she'd felt the pain. She'd wallowed in the violence of the killer's insane thoughts. She believed that the killer was watching Kristie and Stu, but what if she was wrong? Could Stu pass for sane in Kristie's presence for more than a year, while living a secret life filled with hate and violence?

"Maybe if I touch some of his things, as you suggested, I can see more. I'd love to be able to eliminate him as a suspect."

Kristie breathed a sigh of relief. "Great. If you're right about the man who murdered the Huffs watching us, then Stu is in danger, too. He needs to know what's going on so he can protect himself, and us." Again she placed a hand over her belly.

The fact that Kristie was so accepting only made Annie want more fiercely to clear Stu's name.

Someone should be home! He lay on the chilled packed earth beneath the house and listened. The house was silent, and they weren't in the bed-and-breakfast. The place was empty, at the moment. No, they should be *here*.

He was about to slip out from beneath the house and go home, disappointed and very angry, when he heard a car approach. A smile crossed his face. At least one of them was home. Maybe both, but at least one. He hoped it was Kristie. Sometimes she'd hum as she cleaned the house, and she'd even been known to talk to herself. Sometimes he'd pretend that she was talking to him. That he was sitting on her sofa, eating cookies she'd made for him and watching her work. She flittered about, energetic and bright in a way that lit the emptiness inside him. She made the darkness go away, for a while.

The Bentleys were not the first couple he had chosen, but he was beginning to think they were the best. Some couples disappointed him quickly, and he had to kill them before a month had passed. Some had lasted longer—as much as three months.

The Bentleys might set a new record. They were so much in love, and there might be a future baby to consider. It would be like his own child, he imagined. Yes, he might watch the Bentleys for a long time to come.

As long as they didn't disappoint him.

Kristie was not alone. He immediately recognized the other voice overhead as Annie Lockhart's. He would prefer for Kristie to be his and his alone, for a while, but she was a sweet woman who needed her friends.

But why did it have to be Annie? She and that nosy Santana made him nervous. They poked their noses where they did not belong.

If he listened closely, he could hear the voices above his head. Footsteps echoed, and soft voices reached his ears.

"What might work?" Kristie asked. "A toothbrush? Clothing? His favorite chair?"

"I don't know," Annie said, and then she laughed. "Let's save the toothbrush as a last resort."

"Start with clothing," a third voice suggested.

He'd thought the louder thud above was Annie's boots, but apparently it was that bastard Santana. What was he doing here? Could he never let Annie out of his sight? And what did they want with Stu's clothes?

He listened to footsteps above. A few annoying words slipped past him, too soft to discern. And then everything grew quiet. Oh, what he wouldn't give for a glimpse into the house! That would be next. He'd drill a few small holes in the floor one day while Stu and Kristie were not at home, and then he'd be able to see as well as hear.

But now he could not see.

It was Santana who spoke first. "What do you see?" he snapped.

"Love," Annie said, her voice just barely loud enough for him to hear. "Love and…some worry, about money and the new baby."

"I've told him not to worry so much," Kristie said.

Beneath the house, there was a flurry of confusion. Hands turned into tight fists. Stu wasn't here. How could they be talking about him? How could they *see* him?

"Kristie's right," Annie continued. "Stu wouldn't hurt a fly."

"I told you Stu didn't kill the Huffs or anyone else," Kristie said, her voice a combination of indignation and relief.

In the cool of the crawl space, the man who *had* killed the Huffs held his breath. How did they know? He'd suspected that Santana and Annie knew too much, but he couldn't figure out how. How annoying. Obviously they'd told Kristie too much, which meant she and Stu wouldn't be around much longer. Their deaths on top of the Huffs would raise too many questions, which meant he'd have to move again. He'd have to change his name again, and don a new persona for his new neighbors.

Who would he be this time?

"It's not Stu," Annie said. "I'm sure of that. But I feel like the man I've been dreaming about is close. It's like that night we ate supper here, and I felt like his eyes were on me the entire time." She gasped. "Lucky, he's so close, I can…I can almost touch him. He's here. Somehow, he's here."

The man beneath the house scurried toward the small cellar door at the back of the house. Dreams? Feelings? Was it possible that Annie Lockhart was some sort of clairvoyant? *Witch*. That was the word for women like her. If that was true, then he didn't have time to plan. He had to eliminate her and everyone she'd shared her *dreams* with, as soon as possible.

He tried to leave the crawl space quietly, but it was too late. He heard the front door slam, the sound of Santana's footsteps on the front porch.

Running for the woods, the watcher looked back. As he reached the edge of the forest, Lucky Santana rounded the house at a run.

Lucky was standing on the far end of the front porch when he heard the sound from behind the house. It sounded like a wooden door, slamming against the house.

He ran, bounding over the front porch railing and rounding the house with his eyes scanning the overgrown backyard. Movement caught his eye, and he watched as a figure of a man disappeared into the woods.

He increased his speed, drawing his gun as he pursued the man who'd been watching and listening. How much had he seen and heard? Did he know he'd been caught? Yeah, why else would he take the chance of running this way?

The woods were thick, and Lucky wasn't far into them before he knew finding his quarry would be difficult, if not impossible. Especially if the man was familiar with these woods, as he most likely was.

Most terrifying was the possibility that the killer had circled around, and while Lucky searched the woods for a sign of the man's trail, a psycho intent on harming Annie and her friend was making his way back to the house.

Lucky didn't move any slower as he returned to the house. His imagination was working overtime. The women were alone. Annie, who meant more to him than he was willing to admit, and Kristie, who was carrying her first child.

Love was a bitch.

Lucky ran hard, determined to force out the thoughts he didn't want or need with sheer physical force. Annie had been different from the beginning, but he hadn't suspected that she might work her way so completely beneath his skin until it was too late. There were a thousand reasons why the two of them wouldn't work.

And one reason why he wished it could.

He didn't find the women inside the house. They were standing at the back, peeking through a low door that had apparently led the man they were searching for into the crawl space. As he moved closer he saw that Kristie shook, with fear and anger. He couldn't blame her. A man had been under her house, spying on her and her husband. For how long?

Annie was oddly calm now. She knew the intruder—the killer—was gone, and he wasn't headed back. Not now.

Lucky was so relieved to see them both standing there, well and unharmed and foolishly out in the open, that for a moment he couldn't think of anything else. He didn't care that the killer had gotten away. His job was here. His job was Annie.

He grabbed Annie's arm, perhaps a bit more firmly than he should have, given that he had done his best to convince her that he didn't care.

"You're both getting out of here. Stu, too," he added when Kristie began to protest.

Annie and Kristie both argued that they had businesses that could not be abandoned at a moment's notice. There were guests in the bed-and-breakfast, and while Annie had managers in both her stores, those managers were accustomed to having the owner in the shop to handle certain duties.

Lucky barely listened. He didn't care. All that mattered was keeping the women safe. They were his responsibility; only he could save them. Arrangements could be made for the bed-and-breakfast and Annie's stores. For how long? He didn't know. And didn't care, either.

Annie remained oddly calm. She sent Kristie into the house to pack an overnight bag. She explained that Lucky was right, and arrangements could be made. And then, when Kristie was gone, she looked directly into Lucky's eyes.

"It's not your fault," she said softly. One hand came up and touched his cheek.

"I don't know what you're talking about."

"No, I guess you don't." Her fingers rocked against his cheek. "You were nine years old. No one expected you to save your mother."

"I don't know where that came from—"

"Deep," she said, interrupting him with a whisper. "Very deep. Logically you know there was nothing you could do to save your mother from the man who killed her, but everything inside us isn't always logical, no matter how hard we try to make it so. I know that better than anyone. Let it go, Lucky."

"Can we save the psychological touchy-feely crap for another day? At the moment, I'm not worried about saving a woman who's been dead twenty-seven years," he said tersely. "Right now, I'm only concerned with keeping you safe."

"I know," Annie said, and then she rested her cheek against his chest and sighed deeply. "I think I love you, too."

Chapter 15

Lucky promised that within hours Mercerville would be swarming with Benning agents who would continue the search for the killer, probably in a not-so-subtle way. His plan was to get her, Kristie and Stu out of town that very afternoon. Annie wasn't sure where he'd take them, but it was sure to be safe. Nothing else was on his mind.

Sundays in Mercerville were usually quiet. Tourists were traveling in and out, for the most part, so it wasn't the busiest day. Several of the shops were open, at least in the afternoon, since tourism was such a large part of the local economy and weekenders couldn't be discounted.

Annie's Closet was closed on Sunday. The employees liked it that way, and since so much of Annie's business these days was by phone and Internet it didn't affect her too much to be closed for that one day of the week. A few tourists walked the sidewalks, moving in and out of the shops.

Kristie's phone call to her husband had caught Stu in his car and almost home again, and then he was headed back toward town. Lucky was in the front of the store, making phone calls and barking orders. He did that so well.

Annie and Kristie were in the back office of the Mercerville location of Annie's Closet. Annie scribbled several notes for the store manager and paid a few bills that needed to go out within the week. She didn't know how long she'd be away from home. If it was more than a week, she'd have to make other arrangements.

Even though Lucky was determined that she would be leaving town this afternoon, and she was making all the proper preparations, deep inside Annie didn't feel like she was going anywhere. It wasn't a sensation she could explain, any more than she could explain why she dreamed some things and not others, why she could see into the killer's mind and still not know who he was, why she couldn't remember the smell from her vision that was, for some reason, important…

"I have to go to the bathroom," Kristie said, headed for the hallway. "This way?"

"Last door on the right," Annie said as she stuck a stamp on a bill for feathers and sequins that would be used on a collection of holiday purses…if she ever got to them. Right now, she wasn't certain that she would. Too many of the days and weeks that stretched before her were blank. Not yet decided perhaps.

She heard Lucky's voice rise from the front of the store, and that gruff sound made her smile. He loved her. He didn't like the fact much, and it confused him, which he really hated. But she had felt love.

What she didn't know was if that love was enough. She was still odd; he was still wounded. A man like Lucky didn't want a woman to be able to see his weaknesses. He didn't want anyone to know that he was human, with human frailties and fears, just like everyone else.

Suddenly the air in her office turned cold, and Annie shivered. An unexpected aroma filled her head, as if it were real. It was a familiar odor, the one from her vision. *Lemons.* Sweet, tangy, somehow bitter lemons.

Kristie stumbled into the doorway, her face pale, her hands shaking. She wasn't alone.

Wade Nance stood beside her. A knife gripped in one hand pointed into Kristie's back, where Annie had felt the pain of flesh being sliced. In the other hand he held a block of candy.

Lemon fudge.

Annie glanced toward the front room, and Wade shook his head. His ordinary, commonplace, friendly head. He lifted the hand, which gripped the fudge, to his mouth, and touched a finger to his lips, ordering silence. With the blade held at Kristie's back, Annie had no choice but to comply.

He would have no qualms about stabbing Kristie if they didn't do as he said.

"You won't get away with this," Annie whispered. "Lucky is in the front of the store. Hurt either of us, and you won't escape. Where do you think you can go from here?" And how on earth had he gotten past Lucky?

"I'll get out the same way I got in." Wade glanced up. "Did you know that the attics in these old, connected buildings are separated by next to nothing? Making my way from the fudge shop to this place was easy, and by the time anyone knows you two are dead, I'll be back where I belong, selling fudge to the tourists and making small talk. I promise to be devastated when I hear the news."

He guided Kristie into the room and placed the lemon fudge onto the desk where Annie sat. "Make a sound and you'll both be dead before Santana can get here. Trust me, it's a sacrifice I'm willing to make." He gestured to the fudge. "Eat it. I made your favorite flavor."

"What…what's in there?"

"Sugar, butter, lemon flavoring, lemon zest—that's the secret to the recipe, I believe—and of course walnuts. The walnuts have been soaked in a particular rodenticide. Not enough to kill you. Just enough to cause you to become disoriented and weak."

And then, when she was disoriented and weak from ingesting rat poison, Nance would be able to do whatever he wanted. He'd be able to kill her and pose her body—and Kristie's—in whatever way he chose. A robbery. A suicide. A murder…

"You, too," Wade said, giving Kristie a shove toward the desk and the poisoned fudge.

Annie's heart leapt. "Kristie's pregnant. You can't make her eat that…"

"Can't?" he whispered hoarsely. His eyes flashed with a depth of anger she had not been able to see in him in the past. What exactly had she seen when she'd touched Wade's hand?

Emptiness. A vast, cold emptiness he'd been trying for years to fill. If she'd seen the truth on that day, they wouldn't be here. Lucky would've proven that the seemingly harmless man was guilty of murder. He would never have gotten close to Kristie or her. But she hadn't seen the truth. All she could do now was use what she'd felt of this sick man, what she knew of his dark soul, to reach him. Somehow.

"Kristie has done nothing wrong," Annie said. "She hasn't disappointed you. She hasn't hurt you or abandoned you or revealed the kinds of weaknesses that make you angry. She's perfect, isn't she? Pretty and loyal and loving. Why on earth would you want to kill her? She's everything you've been searching for, for such a long time."

"I don't want to kill her," Wade said. "It's all your fault. You and that man, you ruined everything. Why is he here? What brought him here?"

Annie knew she had to drag Wade's attention away from Kristie, just long enough for the pregnant woman to make her escape. She stood, her hands gripping the edge of the desk. The desk and the offered poison fudge were between her and the man who had invaded her dreams. "I brought him here," she confessed. "I dreamed about what you'd done, how you'd killed the Huffs and I brought Lucky here to find you. To stop you. He will, you know. Even if you kill me and Kristie here and now, if you escape through the attic and play innocent when someone tells you that we're dead… they're still going to catch you." She actually had no idea what was going to happen next where Wade was concerned, and she cursed this unreliable ability that had brought her to this place in time.

But she could bluff. "My psychic powers led me to you, and now, with you standing so close, I can see your future in great detail."

She could tell by the terror that bloomed on his face that he believed her.

"Do you want to know what I see?" she asked.

"Yes." Wade shook visibly. "I mean, no! I don't know what your game is. But you don't see anything. You're just…a girl."

"I see that your wife left you for another man," Annie said calmly. "She's not dead, though you prefer to tell people that she is. Some days you wish she was dead. You wish you'd killed her, the way you killed the others."

He went pale. "You're just…guessing."

"I know you're empty inside, and you try again and again to steal other people's happiness, because it's too hard to try again to make your own. If you fail, it will hurt all over again. If other people fail in your stead…" She shrugged her shoulder and glanced down at the poisoned fudge.

"Eat it," Wade commanded.

Annie lifted the fudge from her desk and broke off a small piece. How much could she ingest before she did permanent damage to her body? How much before she was useless and Wade Nance could do with her whatever he wanted? How long before she didn't have the energy to put up a fight, if the opportunity arose?

"Let Kristie go, and I'll take a bite."

"I can't do that," he said. "She'll tell."

"Lock her in the bathroom. It's not like you're actually going to get away with this. You're going to be caught. You're going to prison, where you'll spend the rest of your life in a small, dark, damp cell. Everything there is gray, including you." She tried to sound confident. "I disappointed you, Wade. Kristie didn't. Let her go."

He nodded his head. "Take a bite, and then we'll take her to the rest room."

"You don't want to hurt the baby, do you?" Annie asked.

"No," Wade whispered. "I don't."

Annie held her breath as she popped a small piece of the poisoned fudge into her mouth. The effects were not immediate, but she knew she'd ingested enough to have an effect, possibly within minutes.

From the front room, she heard Lucky's voice. He was still talking on the phone, making arrangements with other Benning agents, collecting some of the information they'd gathered since the last report.

Together she, Wade and Kristie walked away from Lucky, heading to the far rear end of the shop. Annie remained calm. Once Kristie was safe, she'd call out for Lucky. If Nance was planning to kill her anyway, what did she have to lose? At least Kristie and her baby would be safe, and maybe Nance wouldn't kill her before Lucky reached them. He would use that knife, though. She had no doubts about that. Nance examined the rest room to make sure there was no way to escape. This little bathroom didn't even have a window, so there was no way for Kristie to escape or call for help.

He ordered Kristie to sit on the toilet seat and she sat. He pulled a length of rope from inside his jacket, and ordered Annie to tie her friend's hands. He didn't want her making her way up and through the attic, as he had. Annie glanced up. He'd moved one of the ceiling tiles aside. If he had the opportunity to slip out that way again and replace the tile, would anyone think to look in that direction—if she and Kristie were dead and couldn't tell them what had happened?

Kristie was too short to climb to the ceiling, and there was nothing but a toilet for her to climb on. It wasn't tall enough to do the short woman any good at all. Annie tied Kristie's hands, as ordered. When that was done, Wade closed the door on the bound—but safe—woman. In the dimly lit hallway, Annie felt the first effects of the poison. Light-headedness. Not a lot, but certainly enough to alarm her.

She drew in a deep breath to scream—and Nance clapped his hand over her mouth. With only one prisoner in hand, instead of two, he was able to hold her tightly. The knife he held touched her side. "They'll blame him, you know," he whispered. "When they find you and Kristie dead, they'll blame Santana. I have everything planned to the last detail. You'll both be killed in your office, one at a time. No one will think to look in the bathroom for my escape route, and there's no one else here but your lover."

Nance seriously underestimated Lucky and the men

he worked with, if he really thought he could get away with this. That overconfidence was likely the only advantage Annie had, at the moment.

In the past few days she had been able to reach into Lucky so easily. So completely. She heard him—his thoughts, his fear, even his love. Was it possible that he could hear her now?

Annie closed her eyes and reached for the man she loved.

Lucky. Save me.

Lucky paced amid girlie things, talking and listening and making plans to get Annie to safety. Sadie had informed him at the beginning of their phone call that Stu Bentley had been cleared. They'd gone back several years, and found no suspicious deaths in his immediate area. He was exactly what he appeared to be; a quiet man who led an ordinary life.

Days ago Sadie had added Jerry Tinsdale to the list of suspects, at Lucky's insistence, but she'd quickly cleared him. "He's cute," she'd observed unnecessarily, an observation that set Lucky's teeth on edge. How could he be jealous of a manbo who'd dated Annie twice?

One by one his unofficial list of suspects had dwindled to a few, and even then, he couldn't be sure the man he was looking for was on the list. Anyone and everyone was a potential danger.

For now, Lucky was planning to take Annie and the Bentleys to his house near Nashville. He had a decent security system, and Benning agents were already on their way there, ready to take on twenty-four hour guard duty until the danger was past.

Sadie was filling him in on some of the suspects they'd cleared, and how, when a buzzing filled his head. Words followed the buzzing.

Lucky. Save me.

Annie's voice filled his head, and he quickly ended the phone call with Sadie, promising to call her back and disconnecting before she could say anything more.

Lucky drew his gun and turned toward the back room, where Annie was preparing for a few days away from her business, and Kristie watched. The back door at the end of the hallway was dead bolted. There were no windows. There was no way anyone else could be back there.

The voice persisted. *Lucky. Save me.*

He started to call her name as he made his way toward the narrow hallway that led to her office, but something stopped him. Instinct, maybe. Fear, certainly.

He'd always been a big believer in the power of gut instinct. Was that much different from Annie's abilities? Maybe not so much. As he moved toward the employees only section of Annie's Closet, he smelled something sweet. Something lemony. Something bitter. Like the words in his head, they were real and yet more than real.

Maybe he'd lost his mind.

No. It's true. It's me. Trust me, Lucky.

Those words were not as clear as those of the first message. They were messy. Disjointed.

Drugged.

At the entrance to the hallway, he stopped. Soft voices

reached him from halfway down the long hallway, where Annie's office was located. Instead of hearing Annie's and Kristie's voices, as he should, he caught the tail end of a man's soft sentence. He recognized that voice.

Nance. The fudge guy.

The voices came from Annie's office, and Lucky made his way there without making a sound, back to the wall, eyes sharp. He didn't have much time. Since his phone conversation had ended, Nance would wonder about his whereabouts, if he hadn't already. No, for now he was safe. Nance had dismissed Lucky's presence, and was focusing on Annie. He was making her eat…something. He was making her explain how she knew what he'd done. As Lucky himself had in the beginning, Nance wanted logical explanations.

There were none.

Annie's voice had begun to slur. What had Nance given her? How much? Was it too late?

No. Not too late. Not yet. Save me, Lucky.

Lucky spun into the room, took aim and fired a single shot into Nance's knee. The knife the candy maker held dropped from his hand and landed on the floor, and he howled in pain and outrage as he fell down and clutched at his wounded leg.

Realizing what had happened, Nance regained control for a moment and lunged for the knife, but Lucky was faster. He stomped down on Nance's pudgy, soft hand. The hand of a killer?

Yes.

Annie sighed and rested her head on the desk. "It's

about time, Santana," she said, her words slurring slightly.
"I thought you would never get here. " She looked up at
him, her eyes unfocused. "Didn't you hear me?"

"I heard you." Lucky snatched the knife from the
floor, checked Nance quickly for other weapons and
found none, and then he dropped down to his haunches
beside Annie and took her face in his hands. "Kristie?"

"Bathroom," Annie whispered. "Tied up. She's fine."

Lucky lifted the office phone and dialed 911. He
asked for—demanded—the sheriff and an ambulance,
and then ended the call in spite of the operator's insistence that he remain on the line.

"What did he give you?" Lucky asked, studying
what remained of a chunk of lemon fudge on Annie's
messy desk.

"Rat poison, on the walnuts." Annie wrinkled her
nose. "That's just not right, poisoning a woman's
fudge." She sounded indignant, just enough to convince
Lucky that she was going to be all right.

He cradled her in his arms, for the moment. They
didn't have a lot of time. He needed to unlock the front
door for the sheriff and the paramedics, release Kristie
from the bathroom and make a few phone calls.

But not right now.

"You, ah, spoke to me."

"Yeah." Annie gave him a gentle smile.

"Is that…normal?"

"No, it's not at all normal. It's just you, Lucky. Only
you." She looked him in the eye. "I love you."

"You're under the influence," he argued. "You can't
be held accountable for anything you say."

"Fine, ask me later, when I'm not under the influence of…walnuts soaked in rat poison. Poison wine I could understand, but candy? Have I said that's just *wrong?*"

"Yeah, you have."

He liked that "ask me later." It comforted him, in an unexpected way. If Annie saw a later, then that meant she was going to be all right. Nothing else mattered. Nothing.

She closed her eyes, and he took that moment to study her face. The curve of her cheek, the shape of her eyes, the perfectly shaped eyebrows, the perfectly shaped nose and lips.

"You're beautiful," he said. "Even now, with everything that's happening, I look at you and…you're beautiful."

Eyes remaining closed, Annie smiled. "See? You do love me."

He could argue with her, but why argue with a psychic? It would be a losing battle. "Maybe I do," Lucky whispered.

A moment later he glanced at Nance, to make sure the wounded man hadn't moved. He found the man who'd tried to kill Annie sitting on the floor propped against the doorjamb, watching and smiling.

Chapter 16

Annie came awake and opened her eyes to bright light. Was it Monday morning already? No, judging by the direction of the sun, it was Monday afternoon. She'd slept all night and into the day, thanks to the drugs the doctors had given her.

So much of her arrival at the small county hospital was a blur, and given her drugged state she imagined she'd never remember any more clearly what had happened. Well, she'd been more sick than technically drugged. Poisoned, more precisely. She'd been sleeping in a plain, unfashionable hospital gown, which was apparently opened down the back. Lovely.

Her small private room was filled with flowers. Barely thinking about the how or why, she could look at them and tell who'd sent or brought which arrangement. The pink roses were from Kristie and Stu. The unique arrangement of wildflowers had been sent by the girls at the Mercerville shop, and the autumn-colored arrangement was from the employees at her Wears Valley store. There was a small collection of carnations from Jerry, who'd chosen the least expensive arrangement in the florist shop—but she supposed it was the thought that counted.

Of course, Jerry's thought had been that maybe he had a chance, now that the annoying Santana was gone.

Gone. Annie reached for Lucky, in that way she had learned to do, and she knew he wasn't close. Physical proximity was necessary for her ability to work, he'd suggested. If that was the case, then he was nowhere near her or Mercerville, because she couldn't feel him at all.

She did know that he'd left her Drama Queen T-shirt and a pair of cotton pajama bottoms in the closet just a few feet away, in case she woke and wanted to put on something besides what the hospital had provided. Lucky had known she'd hate the shapeless gown, but maybe she shouldn't make too much of that. Who wouldn't?

The man who'd killed the Huffs had been captured, so why could she still see some things? Knowing who'd sent the flowers without looking at the cards, knowing that Lucky had collected her favorite pajamas and then left Mercerville—even though she didn't doubt that he loved her—that shouldn't be possible if the psychic ability she didn't want was asleep once again.

Just great. Maybe she'd exercised her power too often in the past couple of weeks, and like Grams had promised, it was working more powerfully than it had when she'd ignored and denied what she could do. Maybe if she refused to play anymore, it would go away again. Maybe she could push it deep, as she had for so many years.

The door swung in and she held her breath, refusing to hope that her abilities had failed her and Lucky really was close. A handsome man walked into her room…but it wasn't Lucky. Not even close.

"Hi, Jerry."

"How are you feeling?" he asked, flashing a smile.

"Fine, I guess."

Annie tried to reach past the smile to see more of Jerry. Was he really a manbo or had she misjudged him? Did she really want or need a man as complicated and difficult as Lucky Santana in her life? She sighed, as the undeniable truth came to her. Jerry was just as he seemed. He said exactly what he was thinking, always. He had no ulterior motives, no agenda, no deeply seeded demons. He was a simple man, who would one day make some lucky woman a very good husband.

But not her. Dammit, apparently she needed complicated in a man. She needed a man with demons to battle.

She needed Lucky, and he wasn't here.

Jerry pulled a chair to her bedside, twirled it around and sat down backward, his thighs spread wide and his feet planted on the floor. Had he practiced that move, too? Probably.

"Before he left, that Santana guy asked me to keep an eye on you."

Annie's heart lurched. "He did?"

"Yeah. He said he'd feel better if someone stuck around until the doc sent you home."

Annie managed a tight smile of her own. "How thoughtful of him. What happened to Wade Nance?"

Jerry nodded his head in a thoughtful manner, even though there weren't many actual thoughts involved. "He was here at the hospital last night, but they moved him to the infirmary at the jail. Nance is confessing to everything. Well, Nance isn't his real name, but he hasn't given anyone his real name yet so that's what we're calling him for now. Sheriff Buhl called in someone from the FBI, since the murders Nance committed were all over the place and jurisdiction is a problem."

And Lucky hadn't stuck around for any of it. This was his case, his victory, and yet he'd left as soon as possible—probably so he wouldn't have to deal with her any longer. He'd stayed as long as Nance was in the hospital, but once the murderer who'd threatened Annie—and Kristie—was behind bars, Lucky had split.

And why not? He'd done his job. *Save the girl, take what you can get, walk away before things get out of hand.* Wasn't that it? Close enough.

"I sent you some flowers." Jerry nodded to the carnations. "I was going to check out your cabin and find your mama's number and call her, but Santana said I should wait and let you make that decision." He looked vaguely confused. "Don't you want your mama here while you're sick?"

Good heavens, no. "I'll call her in a little while. I should be able to go home soon, so there's no reason for her to make the trip. I'm fine."

"You sure about that?"

"Positive."

Jerry nodded his head and relaxed. "How about I take you out to supper when you're feeling better? It's been a while since we, you know, spent some time together."

In a relationship with Jerry she'd always have the upper hand. She would be in control, and he'd likely do anything she told him to do, without ever questioning her motives.

And he wouldn't be able to break her heart, because she'd never love him the way she loved Lucky.

"Thanks, but I'd better not."

Jerry looked disappointed. He *was* disappointed, but he'd get over it. Soon, if she knew him at all.

"I'm still kinda tired," she said, pulling the sheet that covered her up to her chin. "Do you mind?"

It took Jerry a moment to realize that she was asking him to leave, but when he did he jumped up and slid the chair back to its place. "Sure. You get your rest, and we'll talk later."

Annie wasn't really tired, but she did eventually fall asleep. She didn't dream.

Lucky let loose a stream of profanity that had the new recruits blushing. He'd been here training for a week, and he was beginning to feel like a babysitter.

Building four housed a shooting range, and today they were familiarizing themselves with weapons and shooting at paper targets. A few of the new guys could shoot, but a couple…not so much. He leaned in until his face was very close to that of one of the younger recruits. Miller looked about twelve, but was actually past twenty-one. Not by much. He was a baby, and if Lucky had his way Miller would not make the cut. "If I was being chased by an elephant and you were my backup, I'd be royally screwed, because there's no way in hell you could actually hit it with a bullet!"

The kid went pale. One eyelid twitched. "Um, sir, I don't think a single bullet will stop an elephant…."

"That's not the point!"

Lucky took the kid by the collar. Cal said Miller was great with computers and gadgets, but that wasn't enough. There was no way they could send a kid who couldn't shoot straight into the field. Might as well just line him up now and give him a last meal, a blindfold and a cigarette.

"Sir," Miller said when they were halfway to the tech building, "I can learn to shoot. I do have other qualifications that make me suitable for this job. If you just give me a chance—"

"Why should I?" Lucky snapped. "So you're good with computers. We have Murphy, and there are plenty of geeks out there who—"

Lucky didn't get a chance to say anything else. Miller twisted, dipped and then—with great ease— flipped Lucky over his shoulder and to the ground. The ground came up hard.

For a long moment, Lucky remained on the ground, looking up at trees. Some were evergreens. Others were in the process of changing color. Red, yellow, orange… In his blurred vision they were actually pretty. He felt like he was about a hundred years old.

Miller offered a hand. "Sorry, sir. I didn't mean to

hurt you. I don't want to get kicked out. I want to work here, and I can learn to shoot."

Lucky didn't move. "Who taught you to do that?"

"Mr. Mangino was here last week."

Dante. Figures. Still lying on the ground, Lucky waved a dismissive hand. "Go practice your marksmanship."

"Man, I'm sorry. I really didn't mean to—"

"*Now!*"

The kid ran back toward building four, and Lucky remained on his back. Just as he was about to rise, his cell phone rang. He recognized the number on the caller ID.

"Everything okay?" he asked, instead of saying hello.

"Yeah." Jerry's voice was always the same. A touch excited, a touch dull. How did he manage that? "That's why I called. Annie's really doing well. In the week you've been gone she's made a ton of new purses. Holiday ones, mostly. Lots of red and green and shiny stuff. And lace. And—"

"I don't care about the purses," Lucky said as he moved into a sitting position. "How is she?"

Is she smiling, is she happy, is she still wearing those ugly brown boots? Is she having bad dreams?

"She's…fine. I can't tell that she's any different than she was before," Jerry said.

The dreams had probably stopped, if Annie was happy and back at work, as usual. With the stalking fudge maker—whose real name was Peter Clifford—behind bars and confessing to everything, she was safe, the danger was over and there was no reason for her to continue to suffer with the visions she didn't want.

Clifford had started killing when his wife had left him. He hadn't always used fudge as his method of delivery, but he did have a fondness for a particular brand of rat poison that would leave those who ingested it disoriented and weak. With that commonality in mind, and Clifford's confessions, they were tying together all his murders.

And if not for Annie, he would've gotten away with it all.

"Call me if anything unusual happens," Lucky said.

"Like what?"

Asking Jerry to keep him informed had seemed logical at the time he'd asked. Kristie would read too much into Lucky's inquiries, and she'd likely tell Annie all about the phone calls. The deputy would follow orders. He wouldn't ask too many questions. But man, he was dumb as a rock, and like it or not, Lucky wanted *more*.

Annie was safe. She didn't need to be saved, not anymore. And yet, he hadn't been able to get her out of his mind. He hadn't been able to turn his attentions to another case or another woman.

"Never mind. Obviously, Annie's fine, and I don't need to be checking up on her."

"So, you don't want me to call you anymore?"

What he wanted and what was best for everyone involved were two different things, apparently. "No. No need to call."

When the phone call with Jerry was done, Lucky lay back on the ground to look up at the trees and take a few deep breaths. The kid had caught him off guard, but that was no excuse. His mind was elsewhere, and in this business he couldn't afford to be distracted.

While he was reclining on the ground, Kelly Calhoun—Cal's little sister—approached with a long white envelope in her hands. She stood over him for a moment, then cocked her head and smiled. "Miller?"

"Yeah."

Kelly had been with Benning's since she and her brother had been reunited, four years ago. She'd had a tough life, and it had taken her a while…but she was coming into her own. She was more confident these days, and she smiled more. Now and then, he even caught her watching Murphy in a way that needed no explanation.

She did work in the field, now and then, but lately she'd been in charge of the Benning Agency's bookkeeping. The job agreed with her.

"Payment came in on the Mercerville job." Kelly waved the envelope she held, while Lucky rose to his feet.

"It did, huh?"

"Payment in full, along with a glowing letter of recommendation for you and an extra two thousand dollars. I think it's a tip."

"A…what?"

"You heard me. I don't have any idea how to handle this, from a bookkeeping standpoint."

Lucky snatched the envelope from Kelly's hand. "That's all right. I know exactly how to handle it."

Annie hummed a soft tune as she took the peach cobbler from the oven and placed it on the counter. It took her a moment to recognize the song, and when she did she smiled widely.

She wasn't a huge fan of the oldies, but everyone knew "Someone To Watch Over Me." It might as well be Lucky's theme song.

She'd awakened this morning feeling better than she'd felt in a long time. The nightmares were gone, and had been since the murderer's capture. Whatever psychic abilities she had remained muted—but not dormant, as they had been for so long.

Last week she'd been obsessed with finishing as many holiday handbags as possible, and yesterday afternoon, just before closing, three women on vacation had come in and almost cleaned her out. All their friends would be getting bags for Christmas this year.

As she inhaled deep to enjoy the aroma of the cobbler, the vision that had greeted her this morning as she'd opened her eyes returned.

Lucky, naked and in her bed, the fan whirring over his shoulder.

He was coming back.

She'd dressed in a lightweight sweater, which was perfect for the autumn day, her most comfortable hip-hugger jeans and the boots Lucky said he didn't like—but secretly did. While the cobbler cooled, she fixed her hair and chose earrings and put on a little lip gloss.

And then she went to the front porch to wait. She chose the steps over a rocking chair, since she was much too anxious to relax.

Less than a half hour later, she heard Lucky's car

coming up the hill, and the first of her doubts assaulted her. Sure, she knew he was coming back, but would he stay? Maybe she wasn't meant to see what was to come. Maybe nothing besides the visit to her bed was decided.

But oh, the future held so many wonderful possibilities.

Lucky parked close to the front porch. He slammed the car door as he exited, catching her eye immediately. There was no way he could miss her, since she was sitting between him and the front door, obviously waiting for him.

He'd come to her in his best suit, hair freshly cut, cheeks smooth, shoes polished. He held a familiar envelope in one hand, and as he stalked toward the cabin he shook it at her. "*A tip?* Have you lost your mind?"

"Not recently," she answered with a smile.

He looked at her so hard, she felt that steely glare to her bones. As she watched, the glare softened. "You look good."

"So do you."

"Is everything all right?"

She leaned back, resting her elbows on the step behind her. "Pretty much."

She saw him tense. "Just pretty much? What's wrong?"

"You're not here."

He didn't like that answer, apparently. He immediately changed the subject, tossing the envelope to her like a Frisbee. "What's with this crap? A tip?"

"Is that why you came back? To return my gratuity?"

He snorted. "Gratuity my ass." He took another step

toward the porch, and her. "You're not paying a dime, much less a freakin' *gratuity*. Thanks to you, a serial killer is off the street. That shouldn't come with a bill."

"Thanks. I appreciate it. I guess I can open that Pigeon Forge store after all."

"Or not." Lucky sat beside her, but he didn't touch her.

"What do you mean by that? I've been planning to open a new, bigger store for years, and I finally have the money saved. Why the *or not?*"

Lucky looked down at her, those amber eyes she'd loved from the beginning touching her to the pit of her soul. "I think Nashville would be a much better location for a new store."

Her heart skipped a beat. "Why?"

"Because I'm going to be running the Nashville office, beginning after the first of the year, and the commute from Mercerville would be a bitch."

Annie smiled. The smile was wide and real and unstoppable. "You're going to stay."

"Either that, or you're coming home with me. I don't care which, as long as I can wake up to see your face every morning."

"I have a few bad memories of Nashville, you know," she said, unworried and willing to try anything that would keep her and Lucky together.

"I'll protect you," he promised.

"I know you will." She also knew the good memories they would make would wipe away all the old bad ones. Right now, what had happened there so long ago seemed very, very unimportant.

Lucky finally, *finally* kissed her, and when the kiss

was done, Annie was breathless. She held on to Lucky and rested her head on his shoulder. "I suppose I should be annoyed that you didn't *ask* me if I want to live with you, but…"

"Marry me," he said. "I'm strangely old-fashioned that way. We're getting married."

Annie sighed and smiled some more. "We are?"

"We are. Soon."

Very soon, she suspected. No, she knew. Her psychic abilities might be muted where everyone else was concerned, but with Lucky that wasn't the case. They were forever connected, soul deep and rock solid.

He stood, took her hand and led her into the house. With the door closed behind him, he lifted her off her feet and carried her out of the den, down the hallway and to her bed. He undressed her, and she undressed him and then they fell into the bed naked and hungry. She hadn't known it was possible to want—to *need*—anyone or anything so much.

There was no practiced seduction this time, no teasing or drawn-out foreplay. A few kisses and they were both beyond ready. Lucky guided himself into her and made love to her, rocking in a slow, sensual rhythm that made time stop. Annie closed her eyes and got lost in the sensations they created.

She opened her eyes and caught her breath. This was it. This was the moment she had seen for so long. Lucky above her, the fan whirring slowly, the scar on his shoulder…

They came together, and everything but the beauty of the moment was forgotten. The past didn't matter, and neither did the future. There was only *now*. This moment, this day.

Lucky lowered his head and kissed her, slowly this time. He was sated, for the moment. Relaxed and satisfied and…happy.

"I love you," he whispered.

"I love you, too." She raked her fingers through his hair. Was that it? Was that confession the reason she'd always seen this moment where he was concerned?

She didn't think so. She'd known for a while that he loved her, whether he would actually admit it or not.

A new vision wiped away the old one, and the power of it, the certainty, wiped away everything else.

A little dark-haired, blue-eyed girl who looked like her father and had her mother's gift. A child who would have dreams that were more than dreams, who would know when her daddy was going to be late from work or when her mama was going to burn the cookies. A psychic much more powerful than her mother would ever be. A little girl whose laugh would grab Annie's heart, and Lucky's. A daughter who would be loved, so much, by her parents.

A baby, who would arrive in nine months or so.

Annie laughed and held Lucky close. "So, what do you think about babies?"

"I hear they smell bad," he teased, and then he rose up slightly and looked into her eyes. A moment later, he blinked and uttered an uncertain, "Oh." And then, mere seconds later, he returned her smile. "I'm ready for anything. How about you?"

Anything, love. Anything at all.

* * * * *

Set in darkness beyond the ordinary world.
Passionate tales of life and death.
With characters' lives ruled by laws the everyday
world can't begin to imagine.

Introducing NOCTURNE, *a spine-tingling new line*
from Silhouette Books.

The thrills and chills begin with UNFORGIVEN by
Lindsay McKenna

Plucked from the depths of hell, former military sharp-shooter Reno Manchahi was hired by the government to kill a thief, but he had a mission of his own. Descended from a family of shape-shifters, Reno vowed to get the revenge he'd thirsted for all these years. But his mission went awry when his target turned out to be a powerful seductress, Magdalena Calen Hernandez, who risked everything to battle a potent evil. Suddenly, Reno had to transform himself into a true hero and fight the enemy that threatened them all. He had to become a Warrior for the Light....

Turn the page for a sneak preview of UNFORGIVEN
by Lindsay McKenna.
On sale September 26, wherever books are sold.

Chapter 1

One shot...one kill.

The sixteen-pound sledgehammer came down with such fierce power that the granite boulder shattered instantly. A spray of glittering mica exploded into the air and sparkled momentarily around the man who wielded the tool as if it were a weapon. Sweat ran in rivulets down Reno Manchahi's drawn, intense face. Naked from the waist up, the hot July sun beating down on his back, he hefted the sledgehammer skyward once more. Muscles in his thick forearms leaped and biceps bulged. Even his breath was focused on the boulder. In his mind's eye, he pictured Army General Robert Hampton's fleshy, arrogant fifty-year-old features on the rock's surface. Air exploded from between his lips as he brought the avenging hammer down. The boulder pulverized beneath his funneled hatred.

One shot...one kill...

Nostrils flaring, he inhaled the dank, humid heat and drew it deep into his massive lungs. Revenge allowed Reno to endure his imprisonment at a U.S. Navy brig near San Diego, California. Drops of sweat were flung in all directions as the crack of his sledgehammer claimed a third stone victim. Mouth taut, Reno moved to the next boulder.

The other prisoners in the stone yard gave him a wide berth. They always did. They instinctively felt his simmering hatred, the palpable revenge in his cinnamon-colored eyes, was more than skin-deep.

And they whispered he was different.

Reno enjoyed being a loner for good reason. He came from a medicine family of shape-shifters. But even this secret power had not protected him—or his family. His wife, Ilona, and his three-year-old daughter, Sarah, were dead. Murdered by Army General Hampton in their former home on the USMC base in Camp Pendleton, California. Bitterness thrummed through Reno as he savagely pushed the toe of his scarred leather boot against several smaller pieces of gray granite that were in his way.

The sun beat down upon Manchahi's naked shoulders, grown dark red over time, shouting his half-Apache heritage. With his straight black hair grazing his thick shoulders, copper skin and broad face with high cheekbones, everyone knew he was Indian. When he'd first arrived at the brig, some of the prisoners taunted him and called him Geronimo. Something strange happened to Reno during his fight with the name-calling prisoners. Leaning down after he'd won the scuffle, he'd snarled into each of their bloodied faces that if they were going to call him anything, they would call him *gan,* which was the Apache word for *devil.*

His attackers had been shocked by the wounds on their faces, the deep claw marks. Reno recalled doubling his fist as they'd attacked him en masse. In that split second, he'd gone into an altered state of consciousness. In times of danger, he transformed into a jaguar. A deep, growling sound had emitted from his throat as he defended himself in the three-against-one fracas. It all happened so fast that he thought he had imagined it. He'd seen his hands morph into a forearm and paw, claws extended. The slashes left on the three men's faces after the fight told him he'd begun to shape-shift. A fist made bruises and swelling; not four perfect, deep claw marks. Stunned and anxious, he hid the knowledge of what else he was from these prisoners. Reno's only defense was to make all the prisoners so damned scared of him and remain a loner.

Alone. Yeah, he was alone, all right. The steel hammer swept downward with hellish ferocity. As the granite groaned in protest, Reno shut his eyes for just a moment. Sweat dripped off his nose and square chin.

Straightening, he wiped his furrowed, wet brow and looked into the pale blue sky. What got his attention was the startling cry of a red-tailed hawk as it flew over the brig yard. Squinting, he watched the bird. Reno could make out the rust-colored tail on the hawk. As a kid growing up on the Apache reservation in Arizona, Reno knew that all animals that appeared before him were messengers.

Brother, what message do you bring me? Reno knew one had to ask in order to receive. Allowing the sledge-hammer to drop to his side, he concentrated on the hawk who wheeled in tightening circles above him.

Freedom! the hawk cried in return.

Reno shook his head, his black hair moving against his broad, thickset shoulders. *Freedom? No way, Brother. No way.* Figuring that he was making up the hawk's shrill message, Reno turned away. Back to his rocks. Back to picturing Hampton's smug face.

Freedom!

Look for UNFORGIVEN by Lindsay McKenna, the spine-tingling launch title from Silhouette Nocturne™.
Available September 26, wherever books are sold.

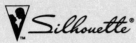
Silhouette®

COMING NEXT MONTH

#1435 JULIET'S LAW—Ruth Wind
Sisters of the Mountain
In a game of cat and mouse, can Juliet Rousseau and Officer Joshua Mad Calf solve a homicide that will prove her sister's innocence, while surviving their growing love for each other?

#1436 UNDERCOVER NIGHTINGALE—Wendy Rosnau
Spy Games
As the hunt for the elusive Chameleon continues, Agent Ash Kelly falls for a mysterious woman dubbed Nightingale, but quickly learns that in this game, appearances are more than deceiving—they can be deadly.

#1437 THE LAST WARRIOR—Kylie Brant
Tribal Police investigator Joseph Youngblood is sent to examine the attempted murder of a photojournalist and soon realizes that the attractive stranger could be the key to uncovering the mysterious deaths of three Navajo youths.

#1438 THE HEART OF A MERCENARY—
Loreth Anne White
Shadow Soldiers
When nurse Sarah Burdett becomes a pawn in a deadly global game, she is thrust into the hardened arms of mercenary Hunter McBride. Now Hunter must battle his desires for Sarah while extracting her and a lethal pathogen out of the Congo in a desperate race against time....

SAVE UP TO $30! SIGN UP TODAY!

INSIDE *Romance*

The complete guide to your favorite
Harlequin®, Silhouette® and Love Inspired® books.

✓ Newsletter ABSOLUTELY FREE! No purchase necessary.

✓ Valuable coupons for future purchases of Harlequin,
  Silhouette and Love Inspired books in every issue!

✓ Special excerpts & previews in each issue. Learn about all
  the hottest titles before they arrive in stores.

✓ No hassle—mailed directly to your door!

✓ Comes complete with a handy shopping checklist
  so you won't miss out on any titles.

- -

SIGN ME UP TO RECEIVE INSIDE ROMANCE
ABSOLUTELY FREE
(Please print clearly)

Name _____

Address _____

City/Town _____ State/Province _____ Zip/Postal Code _____

(098 KKM EJL9)

Please mail this form to:
In the U.S.A.: Inside Romance, P.O. Box 9057, Buffalo, NY 14269-9057
In Canada: Inside Romance, P.O. Box 622, Fort Erie, ON L2A 5X3
OR visit http://www.eHarlequin.com/insideromance

IRNBPA06R   ® and ™ are trademarks owned and used by the trademark owner and/or its licensee.

**Introducing an exciting appearance
by legendary
New York Times bestselling author**

DIANA PALMER
HEARTBREAKER

He's the ultimate bachelor...
but he may have just met
the one woman to change his ways!

Join the drama in the story of a confirmed
bachelor, an amnesiac beauty and their
unexpected passionate romance.

"Diana Palmer is a mesmerizing storyteller
who captures the essence of what
a romance should be." *—Affaire de Coeur*

Heartbreaker *is available from Silhouette Desire
in September 2006.*

nocturne™

Save $1.⁰⁰ off

your purchase of any
Silhouette® Nocturne™ novel.

Receive $1.00 off

any Silhouette® Nocturne™ novel.

Available wherever books are sold, including most bookstores, supermarkets, drugstores and discount stores.

Coupon expires December 1, 2006. Redeemable at participating retail outlets in the U.S. only. Limit one coupon per customer.

5 65373 00076 2 (8100)0 11265

SNCOUPUS

nocturne™

Save $1.⁰⁰ off

your purchase of any
Silhouette® Nocturne™ novel.

Receive $1.00 off
any Silhouette® Nocturne™ novel.

Available wherever books are sold, including most bookstores, supermarkets, drugstores and discount stores.

Coupon expires December 1, 2006. Redeemable at participating retail outlets in Canada only. Limit one coupon per customer.

RETAILER: Harlequin Enterprises Limited will pay the face value of this coupon plus 10.25 cents if submitted by the customer for this specified product only. Any other use constitutes fraud. Coupon is nonassignable. Void if taxed, prohibited or restricted by law. Consumer must pay any government taxes. Mail to Harlequin Enterprises Ltd., P.O. Box 3000, Saint John, New Brunswick E2L 4L3, Canada. Limit one coupon per customer. Valid in Canada only.

52607136

SNCOUPCDN